Easy

Other Books by *mlrpress*

Death Vows

The Death of a Pirate King

The Good Thief

Pulse

Kingsley & I

Man, Oh Man, Writing M/M
for Kinks &Ca$h

Lola Dances

The Ties That Bind

Scared Stiff

Blood Desires

Blood Claim

Genetic Snare

Details of the Hunt

Out There in the Night

The Good Thief

A Bit of Rough

Fearless

Partners In Crime #1 Boy
Meets Body

Partners in Crime #2 I'll Be
Dead for Christmas

The Hell You Say

A Dangerous Thing

Fatal Shadows

SUCKS!

California Creamin'

Bond-Shattering

Love Hurts

Goldsands

Diary of a Hustler

TUSKS!

Easy

ALLY BLUE

mlrpress

Copyright 2008 by Ally Blue

Published by:
MLR Press, LLC
3052 Gaines Waterport Rd.
Albion, NY 14411

Visit ManLoveRomance Press, LLC on the Internet:
www.mlrpress.com

Cover Art by Deana C. Jamroz
Editing by Kris Jacen
Printed in the United States of America.

ISBN# 978-1-934531-62-4

First Edition
2008

The steps creaked ominously under the big man's weight. Roy followed behind him, nearly as excited by the wad of fifties the man had given him as the man himself had been by the boy he'd bought for the night. Just like an angel, the man had said when Roy showed him Sunshine's picture.

"You sure nobody don't come here no more?" the big man grunted, turning to glare suspiciously at Roy. "Awful damn close to the road."

"Street people sleep here in the winter. Summertime, it stays empty. There's better places to hole up. This place's got rats bad." Roy scowled at the rotting walls. "Don't know why you couldn't just have him at my place. It's good enough for everybody else."

"I got a business to run. Can't let nobody catch me comin' out of that damn whorehouse of yours. You think everybody and their grandma don't know what that place is?"

"Whatever you say. You're the one gonna have to dodge the rats."

The big man grunted again. "An' this kid's clean? I ain't wearin' no rubber, and I don't want no diseases."

"Clean as springtime. I make sure my boys stay that way." Roy grabbed the man's meaty shoulder. "And you better not give him nothin', hear me? I'm makin' an exception for you, lettin' you go bareback. You give that boy so much as a fuckin' cold, you'll be damn sorry."

The man grinned back at him as they reached the landing. His teeth, the ones that were left, were stained brown. "I heard you was a mean sumbitch. Heard you cut some kid's tongue out after he gave a customer the clap. That true?"

Roy nodded. "Yep. Little shit lied to me about havin' it. Had to teach 'im a lesson." He pointed a warning finger at the man's face. "You don't think I'd do the same to anybody who spoils one of my boys, you better think again. Got that?"

"I got it." The man laid a hand on the broken doorknob. "He in here?"

"Yep."

"You got 'im tied up like I asked?"

"Yep. But I don't provide no special equipment, and you bring your own lube. You got what you need?"

The man held up the battered black leather satchel he carried. "Oh, yeah. Gon' have me a good time with that boy." He chuckled.

Roy shook his head. Sick bastard, he thought, but didn't say it. "All right, then. Any questions, 'fore I get goin'?"

The big man shook his head. "Nope, reckon I'm set."

Roy nodded grimly. "He's all yours, then. You better be out by mornin', and he better not be damaged. 'Specially the face. You mess up that pretty face, I'll fuckin' kill your ass. That boy's face makes me more money than anybody else I got."

The man looked disappointed, but nodded. "You got it."

They shook hands, and Roy clomped down the stairs, fingering the money in his pocket. His thin face was set into lines of pure greed. A thousand dollars that fat fuck had paid him, just to spend one night with Sunshine. One grand! Roy laughed to himself as he pushed open the door of the decrepit old building and climbed into his Lexus.

He didn't usually like to have his boys tied up. Bondage meant ugly, unprofitable bruises most of the time. But he couldn't say no to one thousand dollars. Hadn't told little Sunshine about the bondage part, of course. Just told him he had a rich customer, one who'd asked for him in particular, because he was so pretty. Sunshine had smiled his sweet, dimpled smile and gone with Roy to the edge of town, to the deserted old house by the river, trusting as a goddamn puppy.

He hadn't thought anything of stripping down, but he'd fought the restraints like a tiger. Lucky Roy had brought some muscle with him, since he'd never have gotten the kid strapped down by himself.

Roy sat behind the wheel and lit a cigarette. He took a long drag, staring up at the boarded-up window of the room where he'd left Sunshine tied spread-eagle to a filthy bare mattress. He sighed. He thought he'd never stop hearing the kid's sobs and curses when he and the other boys left him there. None of his other boys ever acted that way. 'Course, Sunshine wasn't like the other boys. Most kids who worked for Roy were as mean and tough as Roy himself, born and raised to fight for everything.

Sunshine was different. Sunshine smiled at the world, and the world smiled right the fuck back.

A shriek cut the July night in half. Roy clenched his jaw. He looked up at the window again, and thought of the money in his pocket. He rolled up the windows, turned the radio up loud, and drove away.

CHAPTER ONE

Dan Corazon had barely stepped out of his Jeep Thursday morning, and Joe was already on him.

"Dan!" Joe called. "Need you to go pick something up for me."

Dan stifled a groan. He squinted toward the front of the house, where his boss stood beside a tall, slender woman in a tennis skirt. "Where?" he yelled back.

"Milo's. Need some bricks for the barbeque pit."

That explained why Joe had waited for Dan instead of getting one of the other guys to go. Milo had lots of high quality materials for great prices, but he was picky about who he'd sell to. He liked Dan. Anybody else was likely to get a shotgun pointed at them.

"Sure thing," Dan wrinkled his nose. "Dammit," he said under his breath. "There goes the morning."

He shut the door of his battered Jeep and started over to the work site. A guesthouse, of all things. And a patio with a barbeque pit. He shook his head. *That's what you get*, he told himself, *when you work for a home improvement company.*

"Hey, Carlos!"

"*Hola*." Carlos Hernandez wiped sweat from his brow with his forearm, smearing his black hair with sawdust. "What's up?"

"Gotta go to Milo's and get some bricks."

"Bricks? What for?"

"Barbeque pit."

"Aw, man."

"Sorry. I know I just got here, but hey, the boss says go, I go." Dan shrugged.

"No problem, bro."

"Be back soon as I can."

"All right. Oh, hey, Shawna said tell you to come over for dinner Saturday. She's got someone for you to meet."

"Tell her thanks, I'd love to come over for some of her fine cooking, but I don't need her to fix me up."

"She worries about you, man. Says you need a woman." Carlos gave Dan a razor sharp look. "Do you, Dan? You need a woman?"

"'Bye, Carlos."

"Think about it, *amigo!*"

Dan waved over his shoulder as he walked over to the big, open-bed work truck and climbed behind the wheel. He chuckled to himself. Carlos was his best friend in the world. He and Shawna and the kids were just like family to Dan, but he was getting pretty tired of Shawna's constant attempts to find him a nice girl to settle down with. He wondered if she'd still try to fix him up if she knew it wasn't a woman he wanted. He also wondered, not for the first time, if Carlos didn't already know.

He turned on the radio and sang softly along with Emmylou Harris as he drove down the winding road beside the river. The morning sun shone through the trees lining the road and glinted off the flowing brown water. The air was warm, but not yet stiflingly hot. Typical early July weather in the Western North Carolina Mountains. The cool breeze, the green and gold light, the trill of birds and the rush of the river all conspired to send his spirits flying. He rolled the window all the way down and smiled at the morning.

Milo was sitting in his lawn chair in the front yard of his riverside cottage when Dan drove up. He stood, rubbing a hand through his short white hair, and his creased face broke into a wide grin.

"Danny!" Milo called as Dan parked the truck and got out. "How you doing, boy?"

"I'm pretty good, Milo, how about yourself?" Dan grasped Milo's callused hand and they shook.

"Can't complain. What you need today?"

"Bricks. Working on a barbeque pit."

Milo nodded. "Got just what you need around back. Top-quality red brick. Drive the truck on around and we'll load up."

Dan sauntered back over to the truck and hopped in. He was just easing it down the narrow lane to the back of the cottage when the sound of a car engine caught his ear. He glanced over and was surprised to see a white Cadillac pulling away from the deserted house across the street. He could just make out the silhouette of the biggest person he'd ever seen behind the wheel, before the car disappeared around a bend in the road. He frowned as he put the truck in park.

"Hey, Milo," Dan said when Milo came around the side of the house. "What's going on over across the street?" He gestured toward the empty building.

Milo snorted. "Hell if I know, but I sure am glad they left. Kept me up all damn night."

"Doing what? Can't imagine why anyone would wanna spend a night there." He opened the back of the truck and started piling bricks in.

Milo shrugged. "Can't say. Party or something, I guess. You know how them college kids are. They like to go someplace spooky, and I reckon that old place fits the bill all right. But I swear to God, they make that much noise again, I'm calling the cops."

"I only saw the one car leaving." Dan stared thoughtfully at the boarded up house. "What'd you hear last night?"

"Yelling and screaming, mostly." Milo tossed bricks into the truck and furrowed his brow. "Come to think of it, didn't hear no music or nothing though. Huh."

Dan leaned against the truck, staring into space and thinking hard. Something felt wrong.

"I think I'll just run over and check it out," he said after a moment.

"What for?"

"Just because ..." Dan stopped, fumbling for the words to explain something that he couldn't even explain to himself. "Something's not right here, that's all. I'm just gonna check, won't take a minute."

Milo gave him a sharp look. "You be careful. That place is damn near falling down."

"I'll be careful. Be right back."

Dan loped across the shaded road, stopped, and looked up at the boarded windows of the second story. He pushed open the weathered front door. The downstairs was empty, the layers of dust undisturbed. Except for the footprints. Several sets, from the front door, up the stairs, back down and out again. He took a deep breath and started up the stairs.

The steps were narrow and rickety, popping and squealing under his feet. They opened onto a small landing and cramped hallway. A quick check revealed three of the rooms to be empty. The doorway of the fourth, the one closest to the landing, was shut. Dan felt a strange reluctance to open it. He had to wipe his sweaty palms on his jeans before he could turn the knob.

This room was far from empty.

"Shit! Oh, shit." Dan crossed the room in a few long-legged strides.

The boy sprawled face down across the worn and stained mattress was naked, bruised, and far too still. Dan knelt beside the sagging bed. He breathed a sigh of relief when he saw the boy was breathing. At least he wasn't dead. But his eyes were screwed tightly shut, and his fingers dug into the mattress. Dan reached out and gently brushed the tangled, honey-colored curls out of his face.

A soft keening sound escaped the young man's bruised lips. "N-no, no, please don't, please, not again." He drew his arms and legs up, curling into a little ball. His slender body shook.

"Hey, it's okay, I'm not gonna hurt you," Dan said. He stared at the bruises covering the kid's body. Some of them had obviously been made by strong, thick fingers. Raw rope burns circled the boy's wrists and ankles. Bleeding lash marks cut ugly red lines across his back, his thighs, and his pale buttocks. Dan swallowed, fighting nausea. "We need to get you some help, kid."

Dan stood and reached in his jeans pocket for his cell phone. Not there. He swore under his breath when he realized he'd left it in his Jeep. He looked down at the young man on the bed. "What's your name?"

It took a couple of tries for the boy to answer him. "S-S-Stevie," he whispered.

"Stevie. Okay. My name's Dan. Uh, shit. Okay. I'm gonna have to go across the street and call for help, okay?"

Stevie's eyes flew open. Dan stared. The boy had the most beautiful eyes he'd ever seen. Huge, clear, ocean-water-blue eyes, bright and intense. But the look in them was pure panic.

"D-don't leave me, please!" Stevie reached up and clutched at Dan's t-shirt. His grip had the strength of desperation, and Dan couldn't find it in himself to leave him alone, even for a minute. He patted Stevie's hand awkwardly.

"Okay, I won't leave you. But we have to get you out of here and get some help. Do you think you can walk?"

"I ... I, I think ... I think I can."

"Okay, good." He glanced around the room. "Where's your clothes?"

"I, I d-don't ... I don't know. I think, I think maybe h-he took 'em. S-so I c-couldn't run away."

Dan frowned. Whoever "he" was clearly wasn't one of the good guys. He spotted a blanket crumpled on top of a dresser in the corner. He snatched it up and shook the dust out as best he could.

"Here, this'll do for now." He sat down beside Stevie. "Sit up now, Stevie. I'll help you."

Dan wrapped an arm around Stevie's shoulders and managed to get him into a sitting position. Stevie hissed from the pain.

"Where's it hurt?" Dan asked as he wrapped the blanket around Stevie's trembling body.

Stevie darted a fearful glance at him before riveting his gaze to the floor again. "H-he had ... he had t-toys."

Dan stared, horrified, as comprehension hit. A tear slipped through the blood and dirt on Stevie's cheek, and Dan felt a rage like he'd never known before. If he could've gotten hold of whoever did this to this kid, he'd have killed him without a second's hesitation.

"Come on," Dan said, trying to keep his voice from shaking. "Let's get you out of here."

Dan tucked an arm around Stevie's waist and stood up, slowly and carefully so as not to hurt him. Stevie leaned heavily on Dan's shoulder, his matted golden curls brushing Dan's jaw.

"Okay, kiddo?" Dan said.

Stevie nodded. "Yeah." He tilted his head up and stared right into Dan's eyes. "Thanks."

Dan just nodded. The intensity of Stevie's bright blue gaze left him stunned and speechless.

It took several minutes for Dan to get Stevie down the stairs. By the time they reached the front door, Stevie's legs were shaking so hard he could barely stand. Dan stopped and leaned against the door frame, holding Stevie against his chest.

"Okay, Stevie. We just gotta go across the street now, to that house right over there." He nodded toward Milo's cottage. "You think you can make it?"

Stevie smiled up at him, a bright, dimpled smile so at odds with his bruised and battered condition that it tore at Dan's heart.

"Sure," Stevie said. Then his head lolled back, and he sagged in Dan's arms.

Dan lifted him easily, cradling him like a child. *He looks so young*, Dan thought as he gazed down at the mercifully unconscious young man. *What the hell's he doing here?*

"Get on with it, Danny-boy," Dan muttered to himself. He tightened his grip and hurried across the road, yelling for Milo as he went.

CHAPTER TWO

Stevie could hear the argument quite clearly through the thin curtain that separated his little cubicle from the rest of the emergency room. They were trying to keep it quiet. Probably thought he was asleep again. He'd slept for nearly four hours, until the cop had come to talk to him. Slept like the dead, because of the drugs they'd given him for the pain. But now, he was wide awake. He fought off the narcotic haze and tried to pay attention to what they were saying.

"What do you mean, he wasn't attacked?"

Dan. His savior. Jesus in Levis and work boots. Though you usually didn't picture Jesus having lips made for day-long kisses and a body that made your mouth water.

"His words, not mine, believe me. He says everything that happened was consensual."

The cop, a hard-faced, middle-aged woman, looked like she could snap him in half. He knew she only wanted to help, but she scared him a little. He'd learned the hard way that the cops aren't always your friends. Especially if you're a whore.

"Oh, come on!" Stevie could tell Dan was trying to keep his voice down. "You can't tell me that kid agreed to that sort of treatment. He was so scared. You ... you should've seen him."

"I know what you're saying, Mr. Corazon, but I can't do a damn thing about it unless he lets me."

"But there're laws to protect kids, dammit! Even if he agreed to it, there're laws! Right?"

A deep sigh from the cop. "Stevie Sang. 's not a minor. I know he doesn't look it, but he's twenty-two. An adult. I can't make him say he was forced if he doesn't want to."

Silence. Stevie could practically feel Dan's frustration. He shut his eyes. *Any second now*, he thought.

"Mr. Corazon, do you know what Stevie was doing at that old house?"

"No. I wondered. It's not exactly a safe place."

"He was there with a customer. A paying customer. He wouldn't say so, but I'm pretty sure that's what it was. If I had any kind of proof, I'd have to arrest him. But I don't, so I can't."

"What're you talking about?"

"Stevie's a prostitute. Sunshine, they call him, 'cause he's always smiling. God only knows why, but hey, none of my business if he's happy in his work."

A longer silence. Stevie curled up on his side. At least Dan had gotten him here before he found out. At least he'd had a few hours of comfort and safety, something he hadn't had since he came to Asheville. He could handle the things Dan would say about him now. He could handle Dan walking out and leaving him alone. He could.

"That doesn't make it right," Dan said finally. His voice was soft and sad. "Nobody deserves what that boy got. I don't care if … if he was paid or what, there's no way he wanted to be treated like that, and it doesn't make it right."

Oh. Stevie felt like his breath had been stolen.

"Mr. Corazon, I never said it did. But my hands are tied here. He changes his mind, he can let us know, not that we can do much after all the evidence is gone. But we'll try. Now I gotta take off."

"Okay." Dan sounded deflated. "Thanks, officer."

Stevie cracked one eye open. He could see Dan's shadow on the other side of the curtain. Dan's scuffed and dirty work boots and faded jeans showed below the curtain as he paced back and forth outside. Stevie watched him, biting his nails and thinking hard. No one had ever taken care of him like this, not since he started working for Roy, anyhow. It made him feel warm and giddy and utterly terrified.

He pretended to be asleep when Dan shoved the curtain aside. He heard slow, heavy footfalls, then the creaking of a chair. Then, oh, God, Dan's gentle fingers in his hair, petting, stroking his cheek. His breath hitched, and his eyes welled up. He couldn't help it.

"Stevie?"

Dan's voice was very close. Stevie reluctantly opened his eyes, half afraid that Dan would be a dream, that what he'd see would be Roy's cruel face. But no, there was Dan, chocolate eyes and golden-brown skin, rich, dark hair all mussed like he'd just dragged out of bed. His expression radiated concern. Stevie smiled, ignoring the tears rolling down his face.

"Hey, Dan," he said.

"You okay?" Dan brushed a thumb over Stevie's jaw.

"Yeah, I'm fine." Stevie scrubbed at his face, blinked rapidly a few times, and finally got control of his runaway emotions. "Hey, um, thanks. For helping me out. It was really nice of you to bring me here and all; you didn't have to do that."

Dan stared hard at the floor. "Why'd you say that?"

"What?" Stevie asked, though he knew exactly what Dan was asking.

Dan looked back up at him with confusion in his dark eyes. "That what that sicko did to you was something you wanted. How can you say that?"

Stevie shrugged. "Never said I wanted it. I didn't. But he paid, Dan. He paid a thousand dollars for me. One night, to use me like he wanted. That's gonna be more than four hundred bucks for me. I need that money."

"Dammit, Stevie, when I found you ..." Dan broke off, shaking his head. His eyes were haunted. "I've never seen anything like that. Never. And you were scared just about to death. How in the hell can you let that kind of thing happen and not do anything about it?"

Stevie smiled his happy, plastic Sunshine smile. The one that lured men who swore they'd never picked up a hooker before. Men who told him he was beautiful. Men with a need inside, willing to pay plenty for Stevie's pretty face and sweet body to satisfy that need.

Sometimes he wished he'd never learned to smile like that.

"Yeah, well," Stevie said, "I never had a john like that before. He scared me, sure enough. And I can't pretend it didn't hurt. But it's okay now, really. I'm okay. He didn't do any real damage, the doc said."

Dan gave him an indecipherable look. Stevie kept the smile in place. He'd need that mask when Dan got up and walked out in disgust, saying he'd be damned if he ever helped a whore like Stevie again. He'd need it when he left the safety of the ER and went to face Roy and the other boys.

"You got someplace to go?" Dan asked after a minute.

"I got a room downtown. Not much, but it's four walls and a roof." Stevie bit his lip. "I hope I get my cut from last night. I got enough bruises that I might not. Lost income and all that. Most guys don't want a boy that's all bruised and cut up," he added, seeing Dan's brow furrow in confusion.

Now, Stevie thought. *If that doesn't make him leave, nothing will.* They stared at each other, Stevie with his Sunshine smile painted on, Dan with a frown. Finally Dan stood up. Stevie kept smiling.

"'Bye, Dan." He tried to keep the quaver out of his voice. "Thanks for everything, really."

Dan frowned harder. "I'm not leaving. Well, not alone, anyhow."

Stevie's smile slipped a little. "What?"

Dan grinned, and Stevie fought down a jolt of desire. God, who'd have thought the man could get any more gorgeous? But that smile ... that was something Stevie thought he could look at forever and never get tired of it.

"I know you thought you were gonna be rid of me, but you're not. You --" Dan pointed a stern finger at Stevie. "-- are coming home with me."

Stevie's jaw dropped open. "Are you kidding me?"

"Nope." Dan leaned down with his hands on the bed rails. "You can't go back, Stevie. You just can't. Look, I'll help you find a job, and you can stay with me until you make enough to get your own place. A new place, I mean. You go back to where you're living now, you'll end up right back out on the street. You need to get clear of that whole damn life before it kills you."

Dan stopped, eyes wide as if he was surprised by his own impassioned speech. Stevie stared, shocked speechless.

"So," Dan said. "What about it?" He ran a hand through his hair and gave a little half smile that made Stevie want to fall into his arms and stay there until the world ended.

"You serious?" Stevie asked. "You'd really do that?"

Dan shrugged and shuffled his feet. "Yeah, sure."

"Why?"

Dan stared at him in surprise. "Why wouldn't I?"

Stevie laughed. "I'm a whore, Dan. What'll your friends say when they find out you've got a fucking rent boy living with you? What'll your boss say?" He shook his head. "You're awfully nice to offer, but I can't take you up on it. People would start talking bad about you."

Dan's eyes narrowed. "What makes you think I give a damn what anybody says?"

"But ..."

"But nothing. Look, it doesn't matter to me that you've been selling yourself. What matters is what you do from now on. I want to help you out, Stevie. Just ... just let me, huh?"

Stevie knew he should say no, just tell Dan "no, thanks," and go back to his filthy little room and Roy and the street. Back to the life he'd known for the last year, the life Roy said he was born to. But he couldn't do it. He couldn't turn his back on the offer of a hot shower and a safe place to sleep and the possibility of a job that didn't involve spreading his legs for anyone who'd pay. More than that, he couldn't say no to Dan's big velvety eyes and earnest expression.

"Okay," Stevie said. "You talked me into it." He gave Dan his biggest, brightest smile. "You've got yourself a roommate."

CHAPTER THREE

Shit, Dan thought, *I'm in trouble.*

Deep, deep trouble.

He'd had his share of problems in his life. The death of his parents in a car crash when he was seventeen, the struggle to finish school and hold down a job so he wouldn't have to live with a foster family. The life-shattering realization that girls held no attraction for him, but boys did, a fact he'd first discovered at age fourteen and had successfully hidden from his parents and friends. Was still hiding it, as a matter of fact.

But this was the first time trouble had ever walked into his life with honey-gold curls and eyes like the summer sky and the sweetest smile he'd ever seen. Just walked right in, reached down inside him and made him feel things he'd never felt before.

"Hey, Dan?"

Dan jumped at the sound of Stevie's voice. "Yeah?"

"Where's the towels?"

Dan turned around. Stevie stood in the bathroom doorway, naked as the day he was born and dripping wet. Dan gulped.

"In the closet there," he answered, pointing at the small linen closet in the hallway just outside the bathroom. "Sorry, should've told you that before you got in the shower."

Stevie grinned. "No problem." He opened the closet, snagged a giant striped towel, and started drying himself right there in the hall, grimacing a little when the cloth rubbed over the cuts and bruises.

Dan turned back to scanning the interior of his refrigerator, trying desperately to stop seeing Stevie's naked body in his mind's eye. "Uh, you want a beer?"

"Sure." Stevie wandered into the kitchen with the towel wrapped around his hips and took the bottle Dan held out to him. "Thanks."

Dan watched him out of the corner of his eye. The way his smooth, pale throat worked as he swallowed made Dan's skin ache.

"Oh, man, I needed that," Stevie sighed. He set the half-empty bottle down on the counter and turned his wide blue eyes to Dan. "You want me to cook dinner? I'm a good cook. Or, well, I used to be, before. Guess I still am."

"You've got to be kidding me."

"No, really, I am!"

Dan laughed. "I didn't mean that. It's just ..."

"Oh, I get it. Yeah, I know it's early for dinner, but what the hell. Don't know about you, but I'm starved."

"Well, yeah, I'm kind of hungry, too. That's still not what I meant, though."

"What, then?" Stevie leaned his elbows on the counter and gazed guilelessly up at Dan.

Dan shook his head. "Stevie, not eight hours ago I found you naked and beaten and barely able to stand up. You spent a whole night being ... being used by that sick fuck, and now you think you have to cook for me? No. Uh-uh. You're gonna go sit yourself down, put your feet up, and relax while I cook. Got that?"

Stevie smiled, showing deep dimples. "Okay, boss. Thanks."

"No problem." Dan smiled back, trying to keep his eyes on Stevie's face instead of grazing them down that sleek little body. Small pink nipples, hard muscles in a flat belly, hipbones showing above the towel...

Dan shook himself. "Why don't you put some clothes on? You can borrow something of mine if you want."

Stevie laughed. "Yeah, you know what? I think your clothes would probably fall right off me." He unwrapped the towel and padded naked into the living room, dragging the towel behind him. "It's okay. I can go without 'til I get a chance to go get my stuff."

Dan tried to set his beer on the counter and nearly dropped it, because he couldn't tear his eyes from the sight of Stevie's firm little ass and strong, slim legs. He was the most beautiful thing Dan had ever laid eyes on, though the sight of that lovely skin marred by bruises and whip marks made him want to strangle the shithead who'd put them there.

Things went from bad to worse when Stevie spread the towel out on the couch and lay down on it, all pale and golden and absolutely fucking perfect. The sparkle in those enormous blue eyes said that Stevie knew exactly what sort of effect he was having on Dan.

Dan tore his gaze away and started scanning his cabinets for anything that looked like dinner. He made a huge effort and managed to get his brain to think about what to cook instead of what he'd like to be doing at that moment, which was running his hands over all that silky bare skin on display in the next room.

A sudden banging on the door of his apartment destroyed Dan's dogged concentration and made him jump. "Yo, Dan! Open up, *amigo!*"

Carlos. Dan groaned. "Yeah, just a sec!" He raced into the bedroom, pulled a pair of shorts out of a drawer, ran back into the living room and tossed the shorts at Stevie. "Here, put these on."

Stevie obeyed without a word. Something seemed so automatic about it that it tugged at Dan's heart. No one should be that used to doing what other people tell them.

Dan opened the door as soon as Stevie had the shorts on. "Hey, Carlos, what's up?"

"Just checking up on you, after all the excitement this morning." Carlos wandered inside, slapping Dan on the back. His eyebrows went up when he saw Stevie.

"Um, this is Stevie. Stevie, this is Carlos."

Stevie stood, hanging on to the too-big shorts with one hand, and held his other hand out to Carlos. "Hi, Carlos. Nice to meet you."

"Yeah, you, too," Carlos replied. His dark eyes were cool, and Dan could see him sizing Stevie up in his head as they shook hands.

"Want a beer?" Dan asked.

Carlos shook his head. "No, thanks. Just stopped by to see how everything was. And Joe wants to know are you coming to work tomorrow."

"Depends," Dan said. He turned to Stevie. "You gonna be okay on your own here?"

"Oh, sure," Stevie said. "I'll be fine, no problem. You don't need to miss any more work on my account."

Carlos smiled at Stevie. "So, you're the kid Danny rescued, huh? What happened to you? You look like you got beat with a big stick, man."

"Hey, come on, Carlos, leave him alone," Dan protested. "Stevie, you don't have to say anything. Carlos doesn't know how to keep his mouth shut." He smacked Carlos on the head, and Carlos laughed.

"It's okay," Stevie said. "Can't blame him for wanting to know. I mean I do look pretty rough. And you missed a whole day of work because of me, and I'm betting Carlos had to pick up the slack. That right?"

"Yeah." Carlos grinned. "But I'm used to picking up his slack."

"Watch your mouth, boy," Dan threatened.

"Ooo, I'm so scared!" Carlos teased, laughing. "Seriously though, Stevie, I wanna know something, I just ask. You don't wanna say anything, that's no problem, just tell me to mind my own business. I don't take offense."

"It's nothing, anyhow," Stevie said. "I was with somebody, and things got a little out of hand. No big deal. All I needed was a little rest and a cold beer."

He and Carlos both laughed. Dan laughed along with them, but his mind was going ninety miles a minute. Wondering what it was that made Stevie want to pretend that everything was fine, when it so obviously wasn't.

"Okay," Carlos said, "guess I'll head back home. Shawna says she'll expect you on Saturday at six. And hey, Stevie, you come, too, okay? If I know my wife, she'll find a date for you."

Dan looked over at Stevie. "What about it, Stevie? Shawna's the best cook in the city, but her price for letting you eat her food is letting her fix you up."

Stevie laughed. "Hey, I've done worse for less." Dan cringed inwardly, but kept quiet. "Sounds like fun. Thanks for including me, that's awfully nice of you both."

"This is turning into a regular dinner party, isn't it?" Dan said as he walked Carlos to the door. "You tell Shawna we'll be there, but I'm not looking for a relationship, so she'd best not hold her breath over it."

"Tell her that yourself, bro," Carlos said. "Me, I don't wanna bust her bubble. I gotta live with her. Stevie, good to meet you. Later."

Dan shook his head as he shut the door and turned back to Stevie. "Don't let him bug you. He likes to mess with people, but nobody's a better friend than Carlos."

"I can tell," Stevie said. "Must be great to be such good friends with somebody."

Dan glanced sharply at Stevie. He was still smiling, but Dan could see the loneliness peeking out from behind the carefree mask. He wanted to say something comforting and kind to take away that lost look. But he didn't know what to say, so he didn't say anything.

* * * * *

Dan eventually decided on black bean burritos for dinner. He brought a tray piled with burrito fixings, tortilla chips, and Shawna's homemade salsa into the living room. While they ate, he and Stevie sat on the floor, drank beer, and talked.

Dan tried several times to find out more about Stevie. Where he was from, what his family was like, what were his hopes and dreams. And how the hell had he ended up on the street, hustling for some greedy two-bit pimp who kept most of what he made and was perfectly willing to leave him to the tender mercies of sadistic bastards like the one last night. But every time Dan tried to pry it out of him, Stevie would steer the conversation deftly away from himself.

Dan eventually realized that Stevie was much, much better at this game than he was and that he wasn't going to learn shit. So he gave up and answered Stevie's endless questions about himself and his life.

Stevie was amazingly easy to talk to. Before he knew it, Dan was telling him all about himself. His strained relationship with his ultra-macho father -- a political refugee from Nicaragua -- during his growing-up years. That horrible year and a half between his parents' death and finally finding a steady job at the home improvement company where he'd worked for nearly seven years. Everything, in fact, but the one thing, the thing that defined him more and more the harder he tried to hide it.

Not that Stevie didn't try. He seemed to sense that Dan was hiding something, and he kept prodding.

"So, you don't have a girlfriend, huh?" Stevie asked, nibbling on a chip. "I mean I figured you don't, since Shawna's trying to fix you up."

"Nope, no girlfriend."

"So you date around a lot?"

"Not really, no."

"Oh, come on," Stevie laughed. "No way you don't go out. You're hot, man, I know girls have got to be falling all over you."

Dan felt his cheeks flush. "I never noticed."

"Wonder why that is?" Stevie took a long swallow of beer and sat gazing innocently at Dan.

Dan cleared his throat. "What about you?" he asked. "You got a girlfriend? Or, well, I guess you'd have a boyfriend, huh?"

Dan scooped up salsa with his finger, hoping he didn't sound as obvious as he was afraid he did.

Stevie's lips quirked into a wry smile. "Yeah, they're beating my door down, all right. It's every guy's dream to have a whore for a boyfriend."

Dan hunched his shoulders. "Come on, Stevie, don't do that."

"Sorry, Dan. I'm sorry, you're right, I shouldn't talk about that."

"That's not what I meant, Stevie. I just ... I just wish ..." He stopped, unsure how to say what he wanted to say. That Stevie was so much more than a jigsaw of his histories, that he had so much to give. That Dan wanted more than anything to hold him and take care of him and make him feel safe.

"Hey, it's okay." Stevie's smile was bright and brittle this time. "Um, listen, can I ... do you have an extra toothbrush? I'm awfully tired, I'd kind of like to go to sleep if that's okay, and I really ... I need to brush my teeth, there's still ..."

He stopped, looked down at his lap, then back up at Dan. The blue eyes were unguarded this time, and the quiet resignation there made Dan ache inside. He reached a hand out and laid it softly on Stevie's knee.

"What, Stevie?"

"I, um ... it's just that I, I can still ... I can still taste him. In my mouth." Stevie ran a hand through his hair and laughed nervously. "Stupid, I know, I mean after the beer and the food and everything, I shouldn't, but I ... I still can. Yeah, I'm, uh, I'm sorry. Sorry."

"Don't be sorry." Dan scooted closer and took Stevie's hand in his, surprised at his own boldness. "There's an extra toothbrush in the cabinet. You use whatever you need, okay? We can go tomorrow or Saturday and get you some stuff of your own."

Stevie looked up at him, all shyness and uncertainty. "Thanks, Dan. You're the best."

"You're welcome. Now you go on and get all set for bed. I'll pick this stuff up and make up the couch for you, okay?"

Stevie nodded, pushed to his feet, and shuffled off to the bathroom. Dan watched him, feeling a strange sort of twist in his chest. Stevie had been in his life less than a day, but he already felt like the core of Dan's world, though he couldn't have said why.

Dan had known that he was attracted to men for ten years. He'd had a few lovers, always one-night stands, always in secret. Afraid of letting the world know his true nature. But he had a feeling that those days were gone forever in the wake of Stevie's arrival. The thought scared him more than anything ever had.

Yep, he was in trouble all right. And the trouble was, he was already falling for Stevie.

CHAPTER FOUR

Stevie threw the pencil down and buried his face in his hands.

Not a thing. Not a single, solitary, goddamn thing. One hundred and sixty-seven jobs advertised, and not one he had a snowball's chance in hell of getting.

"Well, Sunshine, what the fuck did you expect, huh?" he muttered to himself. "Not many employers looking for someone who can deep-throat ten inches."

He stood up from the kitchen table where he had the morning paper spread out, stretched, and wandered over to the big bay window in the living room. Dan had evidently used the built-in window seat for storing anything he couldn't figure out where else to put, but Stevie had fallen in love with it right away. He'd raked the broken sunglasses, scraps of paper, and unmatched socks into a plastic bag first thing after Dan left for work, and settled on the padded window seat to drink his coffee. Real coffee, ground fresh from dark-roasted beans, with honey and real cream. He couldn't remember the last time he'd tasted anything so good.

Drawing his knees up under his chin, he gazed out the window at the picturesque neighborhood below. Willows, tiger lilies, and little Victorian-style cottages lined the narrow, winding streets. It was so different from the squalid alley outside his tiny room downtown; it might as well have been a different city. Dan had told him that the three-story building was a converted mansion and that every apartment was one of a kind. Carlos and Shawna and their kids lived downstairs, on the second floor.

Dan's third-floor apartment had felt like home to Stevie the second he stepped through the door. It wasn't huge, just a kitchen, living room, bedroom, and small bathroom. But it was clean and comfortable and full of light. No rats, no roaches, no drunks passed out on the stairs. No shivering under his one thin blanket because the radiator had stopped working again.

No more crying himself to sleep at night. No more struggling out of another horrible dream and realizing that the waking was worse than the nightmare.

"That's all over now," Stevie declared to the empty apartment. "All over."

It's never really over, the nagging voice in the back of his brain insisted. *Not for guys like you. Fuck-ups who get kicked out of school, even out of their own families. What sort of person are you if your own family doesn't want you anymore, huh? A whore, that's what. Nothing but a whore. Little Stevie Sunshine, that's all you'll ever be. And one day Dan will realize that, and this shiny little pretend life will be over, and you'll be back to the only thing you're fit for. The only thing anyone could ever want you for.*

"Shut up!" Stevie clamped his hand over his mouth, horrified with himself for yelling it out loud. He lowered his voice to a whisper. "Dan doesn't think that about me. He doesn't."

He scrunched his eyes shut and thought of Dan. The horror on Dan's face when he found Stevie in that dirty, abandoned room. The outrage in his voice over how Stevie had been treated, outrage that hadn't lessened even a little when that cop told him what Stevie did for a living. The expression in Dan's big, soft eyes whenever he looked at him. Tender and protective, heated underneath by a desire he couldn't hide no matter how hard he tried. And he did try, though Stevie couldn't figure out why. He couldn't possibly think Stevie would look down on him for being gay. Stevie figured he didn't have any room to look down on anybody. Least of all Dan, who, in his eyes, was the essence of perfection.

Stevie jumped up and started pacing, bare feet silent on the hardwood floor. He made a face when his movements pulled at the skin of his back. The cuts were scabbing over, and the sharp, dry itch drove him nuts. He rubbed absently at the big purple bruise on his right thigh, trying without success to not think about how he'd gotten that one. The fat man didn't like for him to fight, but he did like for him to scream. And those jelly dildos might look soft and squishy, but it hurt like hell to get hit with one. Especially if it was a particularly big one, and the person swinging it over and over again was very strong and got off by hurting people.

Stevie stopped pacing and started poking around the apartment instead, looking for something to distract himself, to keep his mind off of the fat man and Roy and the hard, cruel boys who made Roy's money for him. He opened the old armoire in the corner and grinned at what he saw. The sound system was state-of-the-art, complete with surround sound via speakers mounted to the walls. Stevie realized he'd seen them the day before, but hadn't really paid much attention to them.

He sure as hell noticed now.

He dug through Dan's CDs, found some he liked, and cranked the volume up.

* * * * *

Stevie was in the kitchen making parmesan chicken, brown rice, and green beans when Dan got home. He squealed in surprise when Dan's face suddenly appeared around the corner.

"You scared me." Stevie laughed. "Didn't hear you come in."

"Hell, I guess not. You've got the sound up so loud it's a wonder the neighbors haven't complained yet." Dan raised his voice to be heard over the music.

Stevie's eyes widened in horror. "Oh, shit, I'm sorry!" He raced into the living room and turned the volume down. "Sorry, guess I wasn't thinking."

He looked up at Dan, half expecting him to be angry. But Dan's dark eyes sparkled with laughter.

"No big deal, I was just picking on you." Dan's gaze flicked down Stevie's body with equal parts amusement and appreciation. "Maybe this is a stupid question, but why in hell are you running around naked?"

"I'm not naked." Stevie hurried back into the kitchen to check the chicken. "I've got an apron on." He smoothed his hands over the red-and-white-checked "Kiss the Cook" apron and grinned.

Dan followed him, nodding thoughtfully. "I can see that." He pulled two beers out of the refrigerator, opened them both and handed Stevie one. "But I can also see your ass hanging out. You a nudist or something?"

Stevie laughed, a little breathlessly because he could feel the heat of Dan's eyes on his bare skin. "Not really. I'm just more comfortable naked, that's all. Especially right now. Clothes kind of hurt."

"Hadn't thought of that." Dan walked over, close enough to touch, and stood looking down at Stevie with worry stamped all over his face. "How're you doing today? You all right?"

Stevie stared up into Dan's eyes, feeling like a love-struck schoolboy. He still found it hard to believe that someone as wonderful as Dan could really look at him like that. Like he was something precious.

"I'm okay," he said, his voice soft and shaky.

"You sure?" Dan rubbed the back of his neck, eyes flickering between the floor and Stevie's face. "I was ... I was worried today. About you. I mean, about all the cuts and bruises and stuff."

Stevie smiled. "They're healing up okay."

They stood staring at each other. Stevie's heart hammered against his ribs. He could smell Dan's skin, heat and sweat and sawdust, and had to fight to keep his arousal from showing. He didn't think Dan was quite ready for that. Though the weight in those brown eyes made him wonder.

The oven timer buzzed, startling them both. Dan blinked, turned away, and took a deep swallow of his beer. Stevie gave the timer an evil glare as he turned it off, opened the oven, and took the chicken out.

"I think I'm gonna shower real quick," Dan said. He glanced sidelong at Stevie. "Won't take me a minute to get clean. I can't wait to get at that food, it smells great."

"It'll be right here when you get done." Stevie smiled, Dan smiled back, and Stevie felt like he might float up to the ceiling.

* * * * *

An hour later, Dan pushed back from the table with a deep sigh and patted his stomach. "Man, that was something else. You could give Shawna a run for her money. You didn't have to cook, you know."

"I wanted to," Stevie said. "You rescued me; the least I could do is put my cooking talent to good use for you."

Dan grinned. "You a chef or something?"

"Naw." Stevie stood up and started clearing the table. "I always liked to cook, though. Joy started teaching me when I was little, and we used to cook together all the time."

"Joy?"

Stevie mentally smacked himself. *Now you've done it*, he thought. *It's all gonna come out now*. He thought about lying, but dismissed the idea immediately. It wouldn't do any good, in the end. He put on his Sunshine smile and forced the words out.

"My nanny, I guess you'd call her. She raised me pretty much all of the time, since Mom and Dad were so busy."

"You had a nanny?" Dan's eyes sparkled with curiosity. "Your parents must be rich."

Stevie nodded. "They own a ski resort in Aspen. They didn't have much time to spend with me, but they tried. And Joy was great."

Silence. Stevie could practically hear the wheels turning in Dan's brain. He turned his back on Dan's questioning eyes and busied himself cleaning up, trying to ignore the hollow feeling in his chest.

"So ... they still live up there, huh?"

"Yeah."

"So ..."

Dan's unspoken questions hung in the air. So, Stevie, why do you rent yourself out? Why do you let a bunch of strangers use you, beat you and humiliate you, all for a few bucks? Why are you out on the street every night instead of tucked safely away in the Rockies with your rich parents? Stevie shut the dishwasher with a loud clang and whirled back around to face Dan.

"So what the fuck am I doing whoring in Asheville, when I could just go back to the good life in Aspen, huh?"

"Stevie, you don't ..."

"They don't want me anymore, Dan. They disowned me. Kicked me right out of the family. My dad ... shit, this is so funny." Stevie laughed, and it sounded a little hysterical to his own ears. "He actually said to me, he said, 'Steven' -- 'cause that's my name, you know, Steven James Sanger. Sounds fancy, doesn't it?"

"Stevie ..."

"He said to me, 'Steven, you are dead to me now.' Just like the fucking Godfather! Isn't that the funniest thing you ever heard?"

"C'mon, Stevie, stop it."

But Stevie couldn't stop. The floodgate was open, and he couldn't stop it now. Part of him desperately wanted to just shut the fuck up, but he couldn't. It all had to come out, and it had to come out now. Now, while he could still go back to Roy. Before he got too used to the warm, golden glow of being cared for. Before Dan became too much a part of him to give up.

"He told me that, and he walked out," Stevie continued. "Him and Mom. And ... and I hitchhiked to Asheville because I didn't have anywhere to go, and I'd seen pictures, and it was so ... it was so pretty, it looked like such a nice place. So I hitched, and I got here, and I looked for a job, but no one would hire me when they found out about my record and stuff. So I didn't have any money, I didn't have a place to live, and Roy found me when I was sleeping in the park downtown, and he said he'd never seen a boy so pretty and wanted to know did I like men, and I said yeah, and he said I could make a couple hundred dollars a night." He met Dan's eyes. "I needed the money, Dan. I hadn't eaten in days. That's why I did it."

Dan stood up, came over and pried Stevie's fingers off of the counter. They were numb from gripping so hard. "Stevie, stop. It's okay."

Stevie stared up at Dan, keeping the Sunshine smile grimly in place in spite of the screaming inside him. "But, Dan, I, I have to tell you, you have to know about me, so then you ... you can ... I'll go, and you won't have to feel bad about it."

Dan's eyes widened. "No, Stevie, you don't have to ..."

"Just hear me out, okay? Before you make up your mind."

"Stevie, please ..."

"The reason my parents disowned me was, I got kicked out of school."

"Lots of kids screw up, especially at that age. They didn't have any right to do that to you."

Stevie bit his lip. "If it was just that, it probably wouldn't have mattered so much. But I got arrested, too. Possession of cocaine. And ... and that's how they found out. About me being gay, I mean."

Dan's thumb rubbed Stevie's knuckles in soft little circles. Stevie curled his fingers around Dan's and made himself go on. "I was seeing the son of the school's president. He didn't want anybody to know he was gay, so we only ever saw each other in secret. His dad was supposed to be out of town, or we never would've been at his house. But there we were, and I was on my knees with Andy's cock in my mouth when his dad walked in on us."

"Shit."

"We'd done a few lines. He liked that, he liked to get wasted first. I think it helped him deal with it." Stevie took a deep breath, ran his free hand through his hair. "Anyway. There we were. Andy told his dad that he was paying me to suck him off. Said I did it to get money to buy coke with. And of course there was the coke right there on the coffee table, so, yeah, Andy's dad called the cops, and they arrested me. My parents bailed me out of jail, and they must've paid somebody off or something, 'cause I only got a couple weeks of community service. But I was out of school and out of the family, without any place to go." He didn't mention that his being gay had more to do with his being kicked out of school than anything else. The small, private Christian college might've forgiven the drugs, but their forgiveness did not extend to homosexuality.

"What about Andy? The bastard."

"They hauled him off, too. I don't know what happened to him." Stevie laughed bitterly. "He told me he loved me. He said when we graduated, we'd move to California together and open a bookstore. I guess it was just too much for him. I guess I wasn't good enough."

"God, Stevie."

"So. There it is." Stevie pulled his hand free from Dan's and stepped back. "If, um, if I could just ... just stay here tonight, I'll go in the morning. I, I washed out the scrub pants the hospital gave me so I can wear those, and my other clothes are at my place, you know, so ... so I'll ..."

The words dried up at last, and Stevie stood staring at the floor, the smile frozen to his face, waiting for Dan to tell him to leave. Waiting to be kicked out again. He didn't look up until Dan came over and laid both hands on his shoulders.

"I told you before, it doesn't matter to me what you've done," Dan said. "Like I said, everybody makes mistakes. There's not one person in this world who hasn't. All that matters is what you do with your life from here on out. And I think you can turn it around."

Stevie stared up at Dan, unbelieving. "What, you mean you're not making me leave?"

"I'm not throwing you out, Stevie. Why's that so hard for you to believe?" Dan's eyes were soft and sweet and full of concern. Stevie could barely look at him.

"But Dan, I don't deserve all this! I've fucked up everything good I ever had. The only thing anybody ever wanted me for was sex. It's all I'm good for. I don't belong here, Dan. I belong out there."

Silence again. Stevie closed his eyes. They flew open again when he felt Dan's big hand cupping his cheek.

"That's not all you're good for." Dan's voice was soft. "Hell, I haven't even known you two whole days yet, and I can see that clear as anything. If you can't see it, you must be stupider than you look buck naked in a damn apron."

Stevie was surprised into laughter. "Yeah, well. Guess I'm stupid."

"No, you're not. But you have to do something about that outfit."

"I could take it off."

Dan's eyes turned heavy, and Stevie held his breath. *Please*, he thought, *please kiss me, please.* He knew Dan wanted to. It was obvious. What wasn't obvious was whether Dan could overcome his fear enough to do it. Stevie had never seen anyone so deeply scared of their own desires.

Dan leaned closer. His hand slid into Stevie's hair. Stevie tilted his face up, lips parting. This, he knew how to do.

For one blazing second, Stevie thought Dan was going to do it. He let his eyes soften, his mouth curve into his most seductive smile. Then Dan blinked, shook his head, and pulled away. Stevie swallowed his disappointment, telling himself that it was okay, it was fine, at least he could stay here, still be around Dan. He told himself it was good enough. More than he deserved, whatever Dan said.

He left the apron on.

CHAPTER FIVE

Dan couldn't sleep. Every time he closed his eyes, all he could see was Stevie, standing there completely naked except for that stupid apron, pouring out his story, his face set into the smile that Dan was beginning to realize was his shield against the world. He'd wanted more than anything to do what the apron said and kiss the damn cook. Kiss away that big, fake smile, kiss away Stevie's belief that he wasn't good enough. Just kiss him and make everything all right, somehow.

He still wasn't sure why he hadn't. Well, yes, he was, if he was honest with himself. He'd wanted to so damn bad, Stevie had obviously wanted him to, and it should've been the easiest thing in the world. But he didn't do it.

Because he was scared.

That was the truth of the matter. He was just plain terrified, when it came down to it. Not of kissing another man, which he'd done before. Not even of being with someone so much more experienced than himself. No, he was afraid because Stevie wasn't just some guy he could fuck and never see again, like the others. Stevie was special. Stevie was someone he wanted to keep in his life. And if things stepped up between them, that would mean changing everything. He'd be laid bare to the world.

And that terrified him.

After squirming around for a couple of hours trying to make his brain stop running in circles, he finally gave up. He kicked the covers off, slid out of bed, and padded silently into the living room. Stevie lay curled up on the couch, sound asleep, with one hand under his head and the other tucked beneath his chin. He looked young and vulnerable and so beautiful it made Dan ache all over.

Dan gently touched Stevie's cheek. Stevie stirred and whimpered in his sleep, scrunching up until his knees almost touched his chin. He was still naked, the blanket wound around his hips. His bare skin glowed in the moonlight.

Dan sank to his knees, reached out and ran his palm over Stevie's shoulder. His skin was smooth and warm and baby soft. Dan let out a shaky breath.

"Stevie," he whispered. "I wish ... I wish I could tell you ..."

He trailed off, unable to finish the thought. Unable to even define what it was he felt. He closed his eyes and leaned close. Stevie smelled like the shampoo Shawna had brought over when she'd found out that Dan washed his hair with soap. A scent like rain and clover, light and fresh and sensual. He rubbed his cheek against Stevie's soft curls, then laid a gentle kiss on his forehead.

"'Night, Stevie," he murmured. He went back to bed and eventually fell asleep, remembering the silken brush of Stevie's hair against his skin.

* * * * *

"Dan! You ready yet?"

"Yeah, I'm coming, hang on."

Dan shrugged his shirt on and buttoned it up. It was Saturday night, time to go down to Carlos and Shawna's for dinner. It seemed like the day had gone by far too quickly. When he woke up that morning and found Stevie in the kitchen, cooking eggs and biscuits in nothing but his skin, Dan had decided enough was enough. He couldn't stand to look at that beautiful body one more minute, not if he couldn't hold and touch and kiss and do all the things he couldn't quite bring himself to do. So he'd borrowed some jeans and a shirt from Carlos for Stevie to wear, and they'd gone shopping.

Stevie, Dan quickly discovered, liked his clothes bright, colorful, and provocative. Luckily for Dan's checkbook, he also had a knack for finding bargains. He'd wanted to go to his place and get the money he'd hidden under a loose floorboard, so he could buy his own clothes, but Dan had talked him out of it. He couldn't help being afraid that if he took Stevie anywhere near that place, he would disappear out of his life forever. That

Stevie would be sucked back into the life he was trying to leave behind and it would destroy him. And Dan didn't think he could stand that.

Dan ran his fingers through his hair and peered critically at his reflection in the mirror. Not bad, he thought. The deep-red shirt Stevie had picked out for him actually looked pretty good. Though he didn't know why it mattered. No matter how nice Shawna's choice of dates for him was, she didn't stand a chance with him. With any luck, she wouldn't be interested.

And yet, he thought as he pulled his shoes on, he'd gotten spiffed up anyhow. Only one possible reason for that.

Stevie.

He wanted to look good for Stevie.

"Boy, you are pathetic," he muttered to himself.

"Hey, quit talking to yourself and hurry up! We're gonna be late."

Stevie's voice was right behind him. Dan jumped, whirled around all set to tease, and promptly forgot what he was going to say. He stood there with his mouth hanging open and stared.

"So, what do you think? Presentable?" Stevie struck a pose and smiled brilliantly.

"Presentable" had to be the understatement of the millennium. Stevie wore a pair of dark gray pants made of something soft and clingy that hugged his body and left not much to the imagination. They hung low on his hips, laced up at the crotch with a strip of black leather. His silk shirt was a pure, clear blue that matched his eyes and gave his skin a luminescent glow. The sleeves hung almost to the ends of his fingers. He'd left the top and bottom buttons undone, allowing tantalizing glimpses of chest and belly when he moved. Dan shook his head and tried to find his voice.

"Wow," he managed finally. "I can't believe those things came from a thrift store."

"Best place to shop," Stevie said. "Unbelievable the things people give away." His blue eyes raked over Dan's body with a heat Dan could feel. "You're looking pretty hot yourself."

Dan could feel the goofy grin spreading over his face, but he couldn't have stopped it even if he'd wanted to. "Well, you picked out some good stuff for me. I'm crap at buying clothes."

Stevie shook his head. The look in his eyes made Dan shake inside. "It's not the clothes. You're just hot, no matter what you wear."

Dan felt the blood rush into his cheeks. He laughed and ran a nervous hand through his hair. "I don't know about that."

"Oh, trust me here, I know a sexy man when I see one. And you," Stevie stepped closer and picked an imaginary thread off of Dan's shirt, "are a damn sexy man."

He let his fingers slide down Dan's chest, barely touching. His smile teased, but his eyes were heavy. Dan's legs turned to rubber. He managed to stay upright by sheer willpower.

"Um. We, uh, we're gonna be late," Dan said. His voice shook.

Stevie bit his lip and pulled his hand away. "Yeah, I think I said that already." He smiled. "C'mon, let's go."

He turned away and headed for the front door. Dan followed him, feeling confused and miserable. *Just tell him, you idiot*, he scolded himself. *He wants you, you want him, what the hell's your problem? He won't wait forever for you to stop being such a pussy. He'll find someone else, and then where'll you be, dumbass?*

Right here, his cowardly inner voice replied. *Right where you've always been, nice and safe and comfortable. So you're alone, so what? It's easier that way.*

"Dan?" Stevie stood holding the front door open, peering back at him with a worried frown. "You okay?"

Dan stared at him, torn between the comfort of familiar lies and the terrifying rush of reaching out for what he truly wanted. When he opened his mouth, he had no idea what would come out.

"Yeah, I'm fine," he said. "Let's go."

* * * * *

When they arrived at Carlos and Shawna's apartment, Dan was surprised to discover that Stevie and Shawna had already met.

"I went up yesterday and introduced myself," Shawna said. "We had a nice talk, didn't we, Stevie?"

"Sure did." Stevie widened his eyes at Dan. "Didn't I tell you that?"

"Must've slipped your mind," Dan arched an eyebrow at Shawna. "I hope he put on clothes for you."

"He didn't, no." Shawna grinned, gray eyes twinkling. "Don't look so horrified, Dan. It's not like he's got anything I haven't seen before."

Stevie laughed and gave Shawna's long auburn ponytail a tug. "Kind of nice to meet someone who's not afraid of a little skin for a change."

Dan shook his head. "Why do I think you two are gonna be hell on wheels every time you get together?"

"Because they are, bro," Carlos said, wandering in from the kitchen at that moment. "I think he's just like her. Only without the temper, maybe, huh?"

Shawna smacked her husband's arm with the oven mitt she still had in her hand. "I'll show you temper, mister."

"Oh, yeah, show me, baby. Papa like." Carlos grabbed her butt in both hands and bit her neck. She squealed.

"Maul me later, horn dog," she said, laughing. "I need to go check the lasagna."

She hurried into the kitchen. Carlos gazed fondly after her. "What a woman."

"Yeah, she's great," Stevie agreed.

"What'd you do with the kids?" Dan wondered as they headed for the living room.

"They're spending the weekend with my parents," Carlos said. "We won't be able to stand them when they get back, I guess."

"Hey, that's what grandparents are for," Stevie said. "Spoiling the children. So, when do the other guests arrive?"

Carlos laughed. "You sound anxious."

Stevie shrugged. "I like meeting new people."

"Oh, no, I know that look, *amigo*. She showed you a picture, didn't she?"

"Maybe." Stevie grinned, eyes sparkling.

"She did." Carlos chuckled. "She loves to play matchmaker. Just go with the flow, man. You don't like this dude, don't worry about it. She'll let him down easy for you."

Stevie laughed, and Dan stared from one to the other, open-mouthed. Carlos slapped his back, grinning. "What's the matter, Danny? You look like you just swallowed a bug."

"I, uh ..." Dan scratched his head. "How did you ..."

"I told Shawna, Einstein," Stevie interrupted. "She asked me if I was seeing anybody, I said no, and she said flat out she was gonna fix me up. So I told her. No point in her inviting a girl over for me, is there? Waste of time for me and her both." He crossed his arms and gave Dan a very pointed look, which Dan did his best to ignore.

"Well, I guess you're right," Dan said. He forced a laugh. "You don't beat around the bush, do you?"

"If somebody's honest with me, I'm honest with them." Stevie stared at Dan, blue eyes challenging.

Carlos frowned. "Did I miss something?"

"No," Stevie and Dan chorused.

Carlos held up his hands. "Okay, okay. Listen, why don't you sit down, and I'll go get the wine, huh?"

"Okay," Dan said. Stevie nodded, and they both sat, Dan on the love seat and Stevie on the big sofa. Carlos headed for the kitchen. He hadn't gotten but a couple of steps when the doorbell rang.

"Carlos, get that, will you?" Shawna called from the kitchen. "I'm just getting the bread out."

"Okay, babe." Carlos sauntered over and opened the front door. Dan heard voices, and a second later, Carlos reappeared with the other two guests in his wake. Dan and Stevie both stood to greet them.

"Okay, everybody," Carlos said. "Guys, this is Shawna's cousin, Melina Hodge, and her friend Jesse Chase. And this is Dan Corazon and Stevie Sanger."

After the initial flurry of handshakes and greetings, Jesse settled on the sofa next to Stevie and Melina sat down next to Dan. He had to admit, if he'd been straight, he would've been all over her. She was a stunning woman, almost his own height, with a curvy figure, long jet-black hair, and pale green eyes.

"So," Jesse said, "you and Stevie are roommates, is that right?" He flipped a strand of light brown hair out of his eyes and smiled blandly at Dan.

"Um, yeah," Dan confirmed. "Stevie just moved in with me the other day, matter of fact."

"I sort of lost my old place," Stevie interjected. "Dan was nice enough to let me share with him until I can find something else." Dan kept quiet and was immensely relieved when Carlos did, too.

Jesse smiled a lazy, artfully seductive smile at Stevie and slid closer to him. "So you're not, like, together?"

Stevie's eyes darted to Dan's face, and he hesitated for a breath. When Dan didn't say anything, he turned back to Jesse with a smile. "No, we're not. We're just friends." He scooted over until his thigh pressed against Jesse's.

Dan felt a stab of jealousy when Jesse laid his hand on Stevie's knee. *Stop it*, he told himself sternly. *You had your chance, and you blew it.*

"Earth to Dan."

Dan started, turned, and remembered Melina. He smiled sheepishly at her. "Sorry, guess my brain's a little fuzzy today."

"No problem," she said. Her dazzling smile probably had men falling at her feet, and here she was wasting her time on someone who couldn't respond to her at all. Dan felt like a heel.

He glanced over at Stevie and Jesse flirting with each other and suddenly wanted out of that room.

"Hey, you want to go out on the balcony?" he said to Melina. "It's really nice out."

"Sure," she said.

He stood, took her hand and helped her to her feet. She linked her arm through his.

"Leaving already?" Carlos asked, coming into the living room with a bottle of wine and six glasses on a tray.

"Just going outside for a minute," Dan said. "Won't be long."

"Take your time," Shawna called. She peeked around the corner. "Hey, Melina, how are you? Jesse, nice to meet you. Excuse me for hiding, I'm just getting everything together."

"Not a problem," Jesse said. "We'll just sit here and get to know each other better." He took Stevie's hand and laced their fingers together. They smiled at one another in a way that said they would definitely be getting to know each other much, much better later on, and that was all Dan could stand.

"Okay, well, the pretty lady and I will be outside if you need us." He strode across the room with Melina on his arm, threw open the double doors and walked gratefully out into the cooling evening.

Melina raised her eyebrows at him. "Why do I get the feeling I'm wasting my time?"

Dan looked at his shoes. "Sorry, Melina. You're a beautiful lady, and you seem really nice, but ..." He trailed off and raised his eyes to hers again.

"But, I'm not exactly what you're looking for," she finished for him.

"I'm sorry."

"Hey, it's okay, I understand. I love Shawna, but she's relentless. All the time, some new guy she wants me to meet." She leaned close. "Don't tell her I said this, but I've told her I had a date before when I didn't, just to get her off my back."

Dan laughed. "Yeah, I can see that. She does the same thing to me. Drives me nuts. I've told her she may as well quit trying to pair me off, but she doesn't listen."

Melina gave him a sly look. "Does she know?"

"Know what?" Dan kept his eyes on the ground.

"Oh, please. You were so jealous just now, I thought you were going to throttle Jesse right in front of everybody."

Dan cleared his throat. "I, I don't know what you mean."

"Yes, you do. Why don't you tell Shawna and Carlos you're gay? They won't care."

Dan opened his mouth to deny it, and couldn't. He let out a deep sigh. "I guess not. But it's not easy to say something like that, even to your best friend. Not when you've spent your whole life hiding it."

Melina took his hand and squeezed. "Dan, the easy thing isn't always the best. You want a chance with Stevie, you're gonna have to come clean."

"Melina, you're a smart lady." Dan smiled at her.

"I know. So you gonna take my great advice?"

"Honestly? I don't know."

Melina slipped her hand through his arm. "I hope you do. Let's go back in now, huh? I think Shawna's putting dinner on the table."

"Yeah, okay." Dan took a deep breath, forced his face into a smile, and ushered Melina inside.

* * * * *

Several hours later, Dan woke with a start at the sound of the front door opening. He was wide awake and reaching for the baseball bat he kept beside the bed before he remembered that he'd left the door unlocked for Stevie. He waited for the adrenaline rush to die down, then headed for the bedroom door.

He figured he should probably just go back to bed and talk to Stevie in the morning, but he didn't think he could wait. He had to see Stevie's face. Had to know if he still had a chance with him. Because Melina was right, he had to come clean if he ever expected to get what he wanted. He smiled to himself. Melina might not be romance material for him, but she was someone he could be completely open with, and he desperately needed that. They'd become instant friends.

Dan heard whispering out in the hall, a soft giggle, and then silence. His stomach dropped into his feet at the thought of what might be happening out there while he cowered in his bedroom. Stevie and Jesse had been all over each other all through dinner, laughing and touching and flirting like crazy. Afterward, Jesse had asked Stevie if he wanted to go out for a few drinks, and Stevie had said yes.

He hadn't even looked at Dan that time.

Dan squared his shoulders and steeled himself to tell Stevie the truth. But when he emerged from the bedroom into the hallway, he stopped, rooted to the spot by what he saw.

Stevie and Jesse stood in the light of the open door, bodies pressed together, caught up in a deep, passionate kiss. Stevie's hands were buried in Jesse's hair; Jesse's cupped Stevie's ass. The soft, wet sounds of lips and tongues sliding together settled like a stone in Dan's chest, inevitable and horribly final.

He backed away and eased the bedroom door shut. After a couple of minutes, more whispers floated from the hall, then the snick of the front door closing and the soft thunk of the deadbolt. He lay, every muscle tense, until he no longer heard the stealthy sounds of Stevie moving around the apartment. Then he buried his face in the pillow and let the tears come.

CHAPTER SIX

It was six-thirty when Stevie arrived at Rainbow Books, where he was supposed to meet Jesse. Half an hour late, he thought grimly. Maybe Jesse wouldn't be too mad. He shoved open the brightly painted door and hurried inside.

"Stevie! Over here!"

Stevie looked around and spotted Jesse on the opposite side of the almost deserted bookstore. He was barely visible in the cushiony embrace of a huge, overstuffed chair. Stevie walked over and plopped down on his lap.

"Hi, gorgeous," Jesse said, kissing Stevie's cheek. "You're late."

"I know, sorry." Stevie pulled Jesse's face up and kissed him on the lips. "Please don't be mad. It's been a fucking long day."

Jesse gave him a tight smile. "I'm sure. So, any luck today?"

"Nope. As usual." Stevie let out a deep sigh and leaned his cheek against Jesse's tousled head. "What the fuck, Jesse? I mean I know I don't really have any experience in anything, but hell, I'm not looking for much. I just need a paycheck."

"Don't worry, you'll find something." Jesse's gray eyes lit up. "Hey, listen to what we talked about today in class! I cannot believe Professor Tally said this, but she did ..."

Stevie tuned out within seconds. He and Jesse had been dating for just over two weeks, and it hadn't taken him long to learn that Jesse's favorite subject, apart from himself, was school. Especially Advanced Unintelligible Crap, or whatever the name of his philosophy class was. Stevie couldn't remember and, frankly, didn't care. He smiled and nodded at what he hoped were the appropriate points in Jesse's monologue and waited for it to be over. Philosophy majors, he'd decided, could talk anyone to death.

When he thought about it, it surprised Stevie that he kept seeing Jesse. He seemed nice enough, in spite of the cruel streak that reared its head from time to time, but his passion for analyzing life was one that Stevie did not share. Maybe it was just the sex that kept him coming back. Jesse might not be a sparkling conversationalist, but he could fuck a guy into a quivering puddle. And Stevie had to admit that it felt good to hold and kiss and make love and know that it meant something more than an anonymous fuck for money.

"Stevie!"

Stevie jumped and bit his lip when he realized Jesse had asked him something and he hadn't even noticed.

"Sorry, Jesse. Guess I'm just tired. What was that?" He put on his most dazzling smile and felt Jesse melt like he always did.

"I just wondered if you want to go get some dinner." Jesse nuzzled Stevie's neck.

"Not tonight, okay? I still need to hit a couple more places before I go home, and I need to get started early tomorrow."

Jesse lifted his head and frowned. "Stevie, you're taking this whole job thing way too seriously. Relax a little."

"Easy for you to say, you have a job."

"Yes, but ..."

"Jesse, this is important to me. I don't want to keep sponging off Dan forever."

"Fine." Jesse sighed. "When you find this all important job, will you have time for me then?"

"Oh, come on, don't be that way. Listen, if I get a job, I can get my own place. That'll be good, huh?" He leaned down and kissed Jesse, a deep, lazy kiss calculated to scramble a man's brains and turn him into putty. "We'll have someplace to go besides your dorm room."

"Uh. Uh-huh." Jesse's eyes were heavy-lidded and glazed. "Damn. Wish we had that right now."

"Sorry."

"Yeah, I know." Jesse leaned his head against the back of the chair and took several deep breaths. "Okay," he said after a couple of minutes, "I think I can stand up now without embarrassing myself."

Stevie laughed as he slid off Jesse's lap, and they both stood. "You're too damn easy, Jesse."

"Only with you." Jesse pulled Stevie into his arms and kissed him. "You do something to me, Stevie."

"I'll do something to you, all right. Later." Stevie smacked Jesse's backside, then pulled away. "I gotta go."

"Okay. I don't like it, but okay."

They linked hands and headed toward the door. Stevie looked curiously around at the cozy shop. Big floor-to-ceiling windows in front flooded the room with sunshine, glazing the sofas, chairs, and bookshelves with golden light. It was marvelously inviting and peaceful, and it amazed him that the place wasn't packed.

"How long's this place been here?" Stevie asked. "I've never heard of it."

"It's been open for about six months. It's owned by a gay couple who moved down here from Chicago." Jesse shook his head. "I buy stuff here whenever I can, just to support them, but I'm scared the place is gonna go under." He leaned down to whisper in Stevie's ear. "Between you and me, I don't think they know much about running a business. This place could be a real happening spot if people just knew about it."

Stevie nodded thoughtfully. "Yeah, it's got great potential, but I think they're gonna have to do more than just advertise. Oh, hang on, let me get a *Mountain X-Press* real quick, huh? They might have some different jobs advertised."

"Listen, I'm heading out, okay? Got schoolwork to do, since we're not going out tonight."

"Jesse, I really am sorry."

"It's okay." Jesse pulled Stevie close and kissed him. "Later."

"Call me tomorrow?"

Jesse smiled over his shoulder and waved as he walked out the door. Stevie headed over to the checkout counter.

The middle-aged man behind the counter put down the book he'd been reading and smiled at Stevie. "Help you, sugar?"

Stevie grinned at him. "Yeah, you carry the *Mountain X-Press?*"

The man nodded toward the other side of the shop. "Over there. The rack's beside the sofa there in front of the window."

"Thanks."

"Any time, sweetie." The man gave Stevie a big, friendly smile before turning back to his book.

Stevie headed toward the sofa, chuckling to himself. The *Mountain X-Press* rack sat half hidden between the plush sofa and a large chair. He picked up one of the papers, then wandered over to a nearby bookshelf. He pulled a book off the shelf and studied the cover.

"Excuse me."

Stevie turned around. A tiny woman with snow-white braids and a pale orange dress that flowed around her ankles stood smiling up at him. He smiled back at her. "Yeah?"

"I wonder if you could help me find something."

Stevie started to tell her he didn't work there, to go ask the man at the counter. Then he stopped. He'd always wanted to run a bookstore. This might be as close as he was ever going to get.

"I'll do my best," he said. "What're you looking for?"

"A new vegan cookbook. I read about it in my Yahoo cooking group. I heard that it has some wonderful tofu recipes." She laughed. "I know this sounds silly, but I can't seem to figure out where things are in here."

"Yeah, I know what you mean." Stevie started walking slowly down the rows, scanning titles as he went. "Do you know who wrote it?"

The woman's brows drew together. "I can't exactly remember. It was an unusual name, though. Indian, I think."

Stevie frowned at the neat lines of book spines. Normally, some books would be turned with the covers facing out, to entice potential buyers. None of these were. It made the shelves monotonous, the sections difficult to identify in spite of the little signs hanging at intervals from the shelves. He only knew he was in the cooking section when he saw the distinctive red-and-white checks of the Betty Crocker cookbook.

"Let's see," he muttered to himself, running a finger along the shelf. "Vegan cookbook, Indian author ... Here, is this it?" He plucked a slender book with a bright green cover off the second shelf down.

The woman's face broke into a sunny smile. "That's it! Thank you so much!"

"No problem, glad I could help."

The woman headed up to the checkout counter with the cookbook under her arm. Stevie glanced around. No one in sight. He pulled out a large, tomato-red book with pictures of grilled vegetables on the cover and turned it around to face forward. The splash of color brightened the whole shelf. He grinned and moved on down the row, picking out various books, and turning them around.

He was so caught up in what he was doing that he didn't notice he wasn't alone anymore until a finger tapped him on the shoulder. He yipped in surprise and whirled around. A tall, rangy man of about fifty stood there, arms crossed, a broad grin spread across his bearded face.

"Enjoying yourself?" the man asked, arching a thick black eyebrow at him.

Stevie bit his lip. "Sorry. I just ... well, I was helping this lady find a cookbook, and I noticed that none of the books were turned out, and you know people are more likely to stop and look if they can see the covers, so ... um ..."

"So, you thought you'd turn some of them around?"

"Yeah." Stevie hung his head and gave the man his best puppy-dog eyes. "Sorry. You work here?"

"Kind of, yes." The man's dark brown eyes sparkled. "I own the place. Well, half of it, anyhow. John and I own it together."

Oh, shit, Stevie thought. *Leave it to me to get caught by the owner.* "I really am sorry. I didn't mean to mess with the merchandise. I'll, um, I'll go now, sorry." He started to leave, eyes glued to the floor from sheer embarrassment.

"No, it's okay," the man said. "No harm done. Matter of fact, I like the books turned around like that." He gave Stevie a thoughtful look. "What is it you do, exactly?"

Stevie glanced up, then dropped his gaze to the floor again. "Um, nothing right now. I'm looking for a job. I kind of quit my last one."

The man stroked his graying beard, still staring at Stevie. "How'd you like to work here?"

Stevie's jaw dropped open. "No way. Really?"

"Sure, why not? John and I love this place, and we really want to make a go of it. But you may have noticed that we're pretty green at running a business."

"Yeah, well ..."

The man laughed. "It's okay; we know we have a lot to learn. You, however, seem to have a talent for presentation, at least. And we need all the help we can get." He stuck his hand out. "I'm Evan, by the way. Evan Schuster. And you are?"

Stevie shook Evan's hand. His grip was strong and rough with calluses. "Stevie Sanger. You serious? You're offering me a job here?"

"If John agrees, yes." Evan started toward the checkout counter, motioning Stevie to follow. "Let's go talk to him."

Stevie followed Evan to the front of the store. His insides shook with a mix of nervousness and excitement. He smiled brightly at John as they approached. John put down his book and smiled back. His face was open and friendly, deep-blue eyes twinkling under an untidy mop of sandy hair streaked with gray.

"Well, hello there, sugar!" he said to Stevie. He raised a pale eyebrow at Evan. "I saw him first, you big ape."

Evan shook his head, trying without much success to look stern. "John, how many times do I have to tell you not to flirt with the help?"

John's eyes went comically wide. "No! Really? We're hiring this one?" He clapped his hands, and Stevie bit back a laugh.

"Only if you agree," Evan said.

"Hey, why don't you guys talk it over in private and call me later?" Stevie said. "I'll give you my number. Or, well, my friend Dan's number. I'm staying with him for a while."

"I don't think so, doll. If Evan says we need you, then we do. I don't know shit about ... you know ..." John waved his hands vaguely in the air. "Business things. I take the money and smile at the customers, and Evan does the important stuff. Don't you, baby? Besides, we could do with something pretty to look at around here." John reached over the counter and grabbed both of Stevie's hands. "But we haven't even been introduced! I'm John Farrell, Evan's much better half. What's your name, sweetness?"

"Stevie Sanger," Stevie said, grinning. "Me and my boyfriend in college used to talk about opening a bookstore someday. It sure would be great to get to work in one."

John laughed. "Honey, you are gonna fit in wonderfully here."

Evan sauntered around to the back of the counter and kissed the top of John's head. "I'm taking Stevie back to the office to fill out the paperwork, you think you can behave until I get back?"

"Baby, you know better than that." John smacked Evan hard on the butt. "Now go away before I have to molest you, hot stuff." He bit Evan's shoulder and gave him a playful shove.

Evan shook his head. "Don't mind him," he said to Stevie as they headed toward a door at the back of the shop. "He'll flirt with anything on two legs, but he's all talk."

"No problem." Stevie smiled. "I think I'm gonna like it here."

* * * * *

"Dan!" Stevie burst through the front door, kicked it shut, raced into the living room and bounced onto the couch, tossing two newspapers and a copy of *Out* magazine on the coffee table. "Dan, I got a job!"

Dan flipped the TV off, laughing. "You did? That's great, Stevie. What is it?"

"I'm gonna be working in a bookstore. It's great, it's called Rainbow Books, it's down on Merrimon, and it's owned by this gay couple, John Farrell and Evan Schuster; they moved here from Chicago, and they're awesome, and damn, I'm so excited!"

"I can tell." Dan smiled, brown eyes shining, and Stevie's heart stuttered just like it always did when Dan smiled at him. "I'm happy for you."

"Thanks. Yeah, me and Jesse were there, Jesse wanted me to meet him there after I got done job hunting, so then when we left, I wanted to stop and get a *Mountain X-Press*, and some lady asked me where this book was, so I helped her find it, and I noticed none of the books were turned around; you couldn't see any of the covers, so I started turning some around, and Evan saw me doing it, and I thought he'd be mad, but he wasn't -- he hired me right on the spot! Can you believe it?"

"Wow." Dan smiled when Stevie finally took a breath. "That's terrific."

"Yeah. I start tomorrow." Stevie bounced in his seat. He couldn't seem to stop grinning. "It's just what I always wanted to do."

"That really is great, Stevie."

Stevie bit his lip. "I don't know how long before I can make enough, but I'll save up and as soon as I have enough money, I'll find my own place, and you won't have to support me anymore."

Dan looked away. "Don't worry about that yet. You can stay here as long as you need to." He reached for his beer and took a sip. "So what'd Jesse have to say?"

Stevie gave Dan a sharp look. Dan's dark eyes were stormy, like they usually were when the subject of Jesse came up. Stevie had wondered at first if Dan was jealous, but had quickly dismissed that idea. Dan was attracted to him, that much was obvious from the beginning, but it was even more obvious that he didn't want a romantic relationship with Stevie. *Because he knows about me*, Stevie thought to himself. *He knows that I sold myself for money, and he doesn't want me.* Stevie ignored the hollow ache that this line of thought always caused and forced himself to go on, a big, not-entirely-fake smile plastered across his face.

"Jesse doesn't know yet. He'd already left before I started talking to Evan."

Dan gave Stevie a thoughtful look. "Have you told him yet?"

Stevie looked away from Dan's face. "I just told you, he wasn't there."

"You know what I mean, Stevie. Have you?" Dan's voice was gentle.

Stevie couldn't look at him. "No."

"You have to tell him."

"I will. When I'm ready."

"Stevie, if you're gonna have a ... a relationship with this guy ..."

"Oh, so now you're giving me relationship advice? That's pretty interesting, coming from you." Stevie met Dan's eyes again, and the hurt there quenched his anger immediately. "I'm sorry, Dan, I didn't mean that."

Dan's mouth quirked into a bitter half-smile. "Yeah, you did. And you're right, I guess. I don't exactly have any business telling anybody else what to do when I can't keep a relationship going myself." He laughed, but there was no humor in it. "Hell, I can't even get one started."

"No, you're right. I know I have to tell Jesse about my past." Stevie held his head up, smiling. "I can do that. Nothing to it, right?"

He kept his fears to himself. The fear of Jesse finding out he was nothing but a whore and walking out on him. He wasn't sure why he cared so much. He didn't love Jesse, didn't even like him all that much, to be truthful. But Jesse was the first guy in ages who'd wanted him just for himself, who wasn't ashamed of him or afraid to hold his hand or kiss him in public, and the thought of Jesse's face twisted with disgust scared him. His gut told him that if Jesse found out, disgust would be the least he could expect.

"If he cares about you, he won't leave you because of that. And if he does leave, he's not worth keeping anyhow."

Stevie stared at Dan, startled. "That's just scary, Dan."

"You're not as hard to figure out as you think."

"I guess not." Stevie reached out and took Dan's hand. "Thanks, Dan. I don't know why you've been so great to me, but I appreciate it."

Dan folded Stevie's hand in both of his, thumb rubbing his knuckles. Something about it made Stevie feel safe and protected. "Stevie, listen. I know you've done some things you're not proud of. That's okay. Everybody's got things like that in their past, things they don't want people to know. You're a good guy, okay? You've got a lot to give the right person, and I think Jesse's damn lucky to have you. Luckier than he deserves, if you want to know the truth."

"You don't like him much. How come?"

Dan shrugged. "Just a feeling, I guess."

Stevie didn't get the chance to find out more. The doorbell rang, and Dan jumped up to answer it. Stevie couldn't decide if he was disappointed or relieved. On the one hand, Dan's obvious deep dislike for Jesse intrigued him, but on the other hand, he wasn't sure he wanted to know.

"Pizza's here!" Dan announced, walking back into the living room balancing a huge pizza box.

"Cool, what kind?" Stevie leaped to his feet and ran to get paper plates and napkins from the cabinet.

"Sausage, tomato, and mushroom."

"Oh, man, that's my favorite!" Stevie handed Dan a plate and started piling pizza onto his own.

"I know," Dan said.

They smiled at each other, and Stevie felt a warm glow inside. He went back to the living room and got the newspapers and magazine off the coffee table. Returning to the kitchen table, he held them out to Dan. "You want to read something?"

"Yeah, whatcha got?"

"Hendersonville paper, *Mountain X-Press*, and *Out* magazine."

Dan chuckled and shook his head. "Hand me the *Mountain X-Press*."

Stevie handed it over, then picked up the Hendersonville paper and opened it with one hand while shoving pizza into his mouth with the other. Halfway through his fourth slice, his eyes went wide, and he nearly choked.

When Stevie started coughing, Dan jumped up, hurried to the sink, and came back again with a glass of water. "Here, drink this."

Stevie took the glass and drank gratefully. "Thanks."

"You okay?"

"Yeah, fine." Stevie wiped tears off his cheeks and smiled sheepishly.

Dan straddled his chair and rested his chin on the back. "So what brought that on?"

Stevie held up the section of paper he'd been reading. Dan frowned at the picture. "Who's that?"

"That's the john who bought me that night. When you found me."

Dan's eyes grew diamond sharp. He snatched the paper out of Stevie's hand and peered closely at the picture. Stevie saw a shudder run through him and smiled grimly. *You don't know the half of it*, he thought.

"Says he's gone missing," Dan said, scanning the short article. "Says he's suspected of dealing in stolen cars through the garage he owns out in Henderson County, and they figure he might've crossed somebody he shouldn't have and that his disappearance is suspicious." He looked up at Stevie. "Can't see how that's bad. Good riddance, if you ask me."

"I sort of agree. Thing is, I'd bet good money it was Roy that did him."

Dan frowned. "Who's Roy? I remember you said that Roy found you when you were explaining how you'd ended up on the street, but you didn't say who he was. Was he your pimp?"

Stevie bit his lip. "Yeah."

Dan's eyes darkened with anger. "That bastard. God, if I could get hold of him, I'd ..." He broke off, took a deep breath. The fact that he could get that worked up over Roy made Stevie feel warm and glowing inside. "What makes you think he did that asshole in? Seems to me they're pretty much two of a kind."

"Roy hasn't seen me since that night. As far as he knows, that guy could've killed me."

Dan set the paper down. His dark eyes burned. "And what would he care? Bastard left you with that sicko, didn't he?"

Stevie nodded. "Yeah. He wouldn't give a shit about me. But the thing is, Roy made lots of money on me, and Roy is all about the money. I would not want to be the customer that lost him one of his most popular boys. You can't even imagine how Roy can be when he's mad."

"So, he'd kill the man because he'd blame him for you disappearing on him?"

"Wouldn't be the first time from what I've heard."

"Damn."

"Yeah. But that guy was doomed from the minute he started hitting me. Nothing makes Roy madder than johns leaving marks. A bruised boy brings in a whole lot less money." Stevie smiled grimly. "Last one that left marks on me got a visit from Roy's enforcers. I've seen him around town; he still has to walk with a cane."

Dan stared thoughtfully at him. "What'll Roy do if he finds you?"

Stevie rubbed a hand over his eyes. "Either he'll kill me, or he'll make me go back. Out of the two, I think I'd rather be dead."

"Stevie, maybe you ought to go to the cops," Dan said. His eyes were clouded with worry.

"Maybe. I don't know. I don't have any proof that he's killed people before, just stuff I've heard from the other boys. And if they arrested him just for pimping, he'd be out in no time."

"But ..."

"And what if Roy finds out I ratted him out?" Stevie interrupted. "He'd kill me for sure, and he wouldn't make it quick, either." He chewed his lip. "I'll have to think it over."

"Okay." Dan reached out and touched Stevie's cheek. "Be careful, huh?"

Stevie managed a smile, in spite of the turmoil Dan's gentle touch caused inside him. "I will. Don't worry about me, Dan, I'll be fine."

"I hope so."

They stared at each other, and Stevie wondered again what exactly was going on in Dan's head. His dark eyes were so tender when he looked at Stevie, so full of concern. And something else, something Stevie was afraid to put a label to, because being wrong would hurt too much.

"All right." Dan stood up, rubbing one hand through his hair like he tended to do when he was nervous. "Uh, guess I'll put up the leftovers now. Unless you want some more?"

Stevie shook his head. Dan gave him a little smile, then picked up the pizza box and took it over to the counter.

Stevie wandered over to the window seat and curled up on it, gazing out at the evening sky without really seeing it. A corner of his mind prodded him like it did now and then, telling him that he couldn't ignore his feelings for Dan forever, that Jesse could never be more than a temporary substitute.

He shut the door firmly on that little nagging voice. *Doesn't matter what I feel,* he told himself. *Dan may not know what he wants, but he knows what he doesn't want, and he doesn't want me. He doesn't want someone who has bent over for fifty bucks, and I don't blame him.*

Dan walked back into the living room, sat down on the couch and turned the TV on. "Wanna watch a movie? *Jaws* is on."

"Sure." Stevie uncurled himself and went to sit beside Dan.

Having Dan's body within inches of his own turned his emotions upside down, made him feel giddy and exhilarated. The swooping rush of it almost drowned out the sick feeling he got whenever he thought of what Jesse was going to say when he found out his boyfriend was a hooker. He hadn't asked questions about the bruises and healing whip marks, not yet, but he was probably wondering. And eventually he'd find out, whether Stevie told him or not.

What scared Stevie as much as anything was, he had no idea how Jesse would react. He couldn't help thinking that the gaping, bloody, razor teeth on the TV screen were somehow prophetic.

CHAPTER SEVEN

Time passed quickly. Too quickly for Dan's taste. Every day he watched Stevie's relationship with Jesse become more and more entrenched, more and more an accepted fact. Normally, he would've said their relationship grew deeper, but it never seemed that way to Dan. He couldn't say how open Jesse was with Stevie, but he knew for a fact that Stevie kept Jesse at arm's length. Not physically, but emotionally. He would've bet his left nut that Jesse had no idea who Stevie really was.

It killed something in him to watch them together, knowing that it might've been him in Stevie's arms if only he hadn't been so damn scared. If only he'd told Stevie how he felt when he had the chance. Before Jesse came along. Somehow, he knew that Stevie would open up to him in way he never did with Jesse. The sense of missed opportunity was almost a physical pain.

The hurt of watching Stevie with someone else was almost negated, though, by seeing how happy Stevie was in his job. In the two months since he'd started working at Rainbow Books, Stevie's smile had lost its plastic look and become genuine. Freed from the virtual slavery of his former life, his natural optimism and outgoing personality shone bright as the September sun. Dan felt he could just sit and watch him for hours on end and never tire of it.

Dan was relieved to see no sign of Jesse when he and Carlos walked into Rainbow Books one Wednesday evening in late September. They'd just gotten off work and had headed over to pick Stevie up.

"Dan!" John called from the register. He handed a bag full of magazines to a customer. "Hi, sweetie!"

"Hey, John." Dan looked around at the crowd of people browsing the shelves and talking or reading in the chairs and sofas. "Pretty busy, huh?"

"Oh, honey, I've barely had time to breathe all day. I love it." John leaned forward on his elbows and gave Carlos a flirtatious smile. "Who's your friend?"

"This is Carlos Hernandez. Carlos, this is John Farrell, one of Stevie's bosses."

"Oh, God, don't call me that," John said, rolling his eyes theatrically. "Evan's the only boss around here." He held a hand out to Carlos. "Hi, Carlos, so nice to meet you." He glanced at Dan without letting go of Carlos's hand. "Where've you been hiding him, Danny? He's cute."

Carlos laughed. "Sorry, *amigo*, I'm married. Nice to meet you, though."

"Doesn't Evan get tired of you flirting with every guy that comes in here, John?" Dan asked, grinning.

"He loves me for my sluttish self, sweetie." John waved a hand toward the back of the store. "Stevie's in the back someplace, if you're looking for him, and I know you are. He's sorting through the stuff that came in today. We just got in a shipment of books about how to do Halloween right. You know, costumes, parties, that sort of thing. He's trying to work out which are the best ones to display."

Carlos looked thoughtful. "Do you have any that tell you how to make Gomez and Morticia costumes? My wife wants to do that for Halloween, but she doesn't like to buy those canned costumes in the shops. She likes to make them herself."

"Sounds hot, sugar, but I have no idea." John said. "Ask Stevie, he'll know."

"Thanks, bro." Carlos smiled over his shoulder at John, then followed Dan toward the back of the store. He looked around with wide eyes. "Wow, nice place. I like the murals on the walls."

Dan nodded, glancing up at the paintings of rainbows, moons and stars, and various fanciful creatures decorating the walls and ceiling. "Yeah, that was Stevie's idea. So was rearranging the couches and chairs in circles so people could sit and talk. He's helped them fix the place up a lot."

Carlos gave Dan a sly look. "He's a nice kid."

"Yep."

"Talented, too."

"Uh-huh."

"And he's a damn good cook. Shawna's gotten some great recipes from him."

Dan stopped, crossed his arms, and scowled at Carlos. "Just what are you trying to say?"

"Nothing, bro. Just that Stevie's a nice kid. I like him. So does Shawna."

"That's great, I'm glad. So?"

"So, I'm just saying. That's all."

Dan narrowed his eyes. He had a feeling that Carlos knew. Not just about him being gay, but about his feelings for Stevie as well. Something in those dark eyes begged him to say it.

He wanted to, badly. The burden of secrets was becoming unbearable lately. Telling Carlos would be such a relief, and in his heart, he knew he wouldn't be judged. Carlos would accept the news -- if it even was news to him -- with his usual matter-of-fact calm. Dan nodded to himself. He glanced around at the people browsing among the shelves. No one was paying them any attention.

"Carlos," he said, leaning closer and speaking barely above a whisper, "I need to tell you something. It ... It's kind of hard for me to say this." He stopped, wiping his sweaty palms on his jeans. His heart raced, and his mouth was bone dry.

"You can tell me anything, *hermano*. Go ahead."

He knows, Dan thought. *He knows already, all you have to do is say it*. "Okay. Carlos, I ..."

Stevie came around the corner at that moment, cutting Dan's words short. Dan snapped his mouth shut so fast he bit his tongue. The lancing pain dissipated the rush of fear from Stevie walking in on his impending confession. He forced what he hoped was a casual smile to his face.

"Hey, Stevie," he said. "You ready to go?"

"Hi, Dan. Hi, Carlos. I'm almost ready; give me just another sec."

Stevie wore white jeans that looked like they'd been painted on and a long-sleeved lavender t-shirt with a rainbow embroidered across the chest. Dan knew for a fact that it was a girl's shirt, because he'd been there when Stevie'd bought it. Some guys would've looked either horribly feminine or just plain weird in something like that. Not Stevie. He looked relaxed and comfortable and unmistakably male. Dan bit his lip and fought down a rush of desire even stronger than what he'd become used to over the last few weeks.

"Take your time, bro." Carlos plopped down in a nearby chair. "We'll wait."

"Okay. I won't be long." Stevie gazed up at Dan, smiling. "You've got a smudge on your face, Dan. Here, let me get it."

Dan started to protest. But before he could make a sound, Stevie was standing a breath away, one hand on Dan's chest while he balanced on tiptoe to peer at Dan's face. He wet the pad of his thumb with a quick swipe of his tongue and rubbed at a place on Dan's left cheek. Dan swallowed his heart back down. Stevie's wide blue eyes stared into his, soft red lips slightly parted, and for one electric moment Dan thought Stevie was going to kiss him. His knees turned to jelly at the thought. Then Stevie stepped back, and the moment passed.

"Be right back." Voice soft and husky, Stevie turned and hurried back behind the shelf.

Dan fell into the nearest chair and tried to collect his wits. He looked over at Carlos, who raised a knowing eyebrow at him. But the time for talking had passed, for now at least. Maybe later, Dan promised himself.

Carlos leaned back in the chair, singing softly in Spanish. Dan rubbed both hands over his face. His fingers lingered on the spot where Stevie had touched him. He could still feel Stevie's thumb on his cheek, could still smell Stevie's skin, fresh and sweet as new hay. When he closed his eyes, he could see Stevie's face again, only inches away, that beautiful, ripe mouth so close he could almost taste it. He imagined Stevie would taste tart and sweet, like tangerines.

A hand landed on Dan's shoulder, and he jumped. He opened his eyes. Evan stood over him, smiling his wide smile.

"You okay, Dan?" Evan said. "You're a little flushed."

"Yeah, I'm fine," Dan answered. "It was hot out today, that's all. We were working all day out in the sun." Carlos gave him a look, and he flushed bright red. "Evan, this is my good friend Carlos Hernandez. Carlos, this is Evan Schuster."

"Carlos, it's a pleasure," Evan said, holding out his hand.

"Same here." Carlos stood and they shook. "Hey, you and John want to come over for dinner Friday night? Me and my wife, Shawna, are having a little party."

"We wouldn't want to impose. Your wife might not like that."

"Naw, she's wanted to meet you guys. She'll hurt me if she finds out I was over here and didn't invite you."

"It's true," Dan chimed in. "There's nobody friendlier than Shawna, and she's the best cook you'll ever meet."

"Next to me," Stevie added, emerging from around the corner.

"Right. Sorry." Dan grinned at Evan. "Stevie's making key lime pies for dessert Friday. You haven't lived until you've had some of that."

Evan raised his eyebrows at Stevie. "Oh, so you cook as well, do you? I see you've been holding out on us."

Stevie ducked his head and peered up at Evan from behind a veil of golden curls. With that sheepish little smile, hands shoved into his back pockets, he looked like a kid caught sneaking cookies before dinner. It made Dan's chest ache.

"It never came up," Stevie said.

Even stood stroking his beard thoughtfully. "That's true. But now that I've found you out, Stevie, I'd like to talk to you sometime about an idea I have."

"You need me now? I can take the bus home if you guys don't want to wait for me, Dan."

"No, no, that's not necessary," Evan said hastily. "I have some other things I need to do before we close tonight, anyway."

"Okay," Stevie said. "Well, I guess I'm ready, then. Evan, I'll come in early tomorrow if that's okay, and we'll talk."

"That'll be fine," Evan said. "See you in the morning, then. 'Bye, guys. Carlos, great to meet you, and thanks very much for the invitation. John and I would love to come. Thank Shawna for me, as well."

"Sure thing," Carlos said. "See you then."

Evan went back into the office, and Dan, Carlos, and Stevie headed for the front door. They waved and called good-bye to John as they left. Stevie pushed the door open, and they stepped out into the cool of an early fall evening.

Dan took a deep breath. The air smelled like sunshine and the day's lingering heat, tinged with a sharpness that spoke of sweater weather to come. That smell, the scent of the dying year, always made him feel nostalgic and a little blue. The way the fragrant breeze tugged winding strands of gold across Stevie's neck made him feel other things. He discreetly adjusted himself and tried not to see the way Stevie's ass moved in those skin-tight jeans.

"C'mon, Dan!" Stevie called over his shoulder. He brushed the tangled curls out of his eyes, laughing, blue eyes shining with a joy that seemed to radiate from him all the time these days.

"Yeah, coming."

Dan lengthened his stride to catch up and was soon walking by Stevie's side. Stevie smiled up at him, and the deepening dusk seemed to brighten. Dan swallowed around the sudden lump in his throat. He may have missed his chance with Stevie, but he knew right then that what he felt wasn't going away any time soon. Maybe not ever. He hoped the sight of that sunny smile, the unquenchable spark in those clear blue eyes, would be enough to keep him going. It had to be. Because he sure as hell wasn't getting anything else. Not with Jesse in the picture.

And he didn't see any hope of getting Jesse out of the picture.

"Dan?"

Stevie's voice was soft, concerned. Dan looked down at him and made himself smile. "Yeah?"

"What's wrong?"

"Nothing. Just tired, is all. Had a long day."

"You sure?" Stevie stopped walking and took both of Dan's hands in his, sending Dan's pulse racing. "You seem sad."

Dan glanced over at Carlos. He'd gone ahead to his pickup truck and was making a great show of unlocking the door. Giving Dan and Stevie some time alone. *Oh, yeah*, Dan thought, *he knows.*

"It's just this time of year, I guess," Dan said finally. "Always gives me kind of a homesick feeling, if you know what I mean."

"Yeah, I think I do." Stevie squeezed his hands. "C'mon, let's go home. We can be homesick together."

He pulled away, keeping one hand linked through Dan's. Dan tried to walk slowly. He knew he'd only have a few seconds to savor the feel of Stevie's fingers curled around his, and he wanted to make it last.

It didn't last nearly long enough.

CHAPTER EIGHT

Stevie figured it was John's doing that he got off early Friday. They'd gotten to be fast friends over the last few weeks, and John was always ready to help him out. Or maybe Evan was just that eager for key lime pie. Whatever the reason, when three o'clock rolled around, he was out the door and on the bus, headed home.

He let himself into Dan's apartment, filled the six-disc CD player with the Placebo collection he'd re-bought himself with his first paycheck, and cranked up the volume. He'd had to sell all his CDs his first month in Asheville and was slowly rebuilding his collection. The sounds of the music he used to take for granted in college thrilled him and made his whole body tingle with sheer happiness. He kicked his shoes off, stripped down to hot-pink boxer briefs, and sang along while he cooked.

He was wiping spatters of condensed milk off the counter and gyrating to the beat of "Days Before You Came," singing at the top of his voice, when he heard Dan's throaty chuckle behind him.

"Stevie, why is it the minute you get through this door, you start stripping?"

Stevie turned around and grinned. "Hey, be glad I've got underwear on. I only wear that much for you, you know." He danced up to Dan, threw both arms around his neck, and rolled his hips suggestively against Dan's thigh. "Pies'll be ready in a few. Man, this is gonna be fun!"

Dan laughed, his voice rough and a little breathless. "Uh. Yeah. Well, good." He licked his lips, holding both hands on Stevie's sides, barely touching, making Stevie's skin spark. "I, um ... I better go shower."

"Aw, don't," Stevie pouted. "Stay and dance with me." He pressed closer, giving Dan a lazy smile.

Dan's eyes darkened, his lips parted, cheeks flushing. "Um. I ... I smell."

"I like how you smell," Stevie said. He did, too. Heat and sweat and fresh-cut wood, making his brain buzz with need. He rubbed his cheek against Dan's sweaty t-shirt.

"Well, I don't." Dan pushed Stevie gently away and backed up, wiping moisture from his upper lip. "I, uh, I'll just ... yeah." He turned and stumbled toward the bathroom.

Stevie watched him, a little smile on his lips. He knew how wrong it was that he was always finding excuses to touch Dan, to get close to him, but he couldn't help it. Seeing the heavy look that thickened those dark eyes at his touch made Stevie feel hot all over. He couldn't get enough of it. Especially since he figured that's all he'd ever have.

"Stupid, Sunshine," he said softly to himself. "Stupid, stupid, stupid." He let out a deep sigh and turned back to his cooking.

* * * * *

A couple of hours later, clean and dressed and loaded down with four pies, Dan and Stevie headed down to the big backyard where Carlos and Shawna were holding their party. Stevie took a deep breath of cool, fragrant air and laughed out loud for sheer joy. The last few weeks had been some of the happiest he could remember, in spite of the empty place inside him that he knew no one but Dan could ever fill.

"Hey, guys!" Shawna bounded over, vibrantly pretty in faded jeans and an emerald-green sweater that made her hair flame. "God, those look fabulous!" She took a pie from each of them and led them to the food table.

"So does this," Dan said, gesturing at the laden table. "You must've been cooking all day."

"Not really. Most of it's pretty easy to make, and of course I've got Carlos on the grill." Shawna waved at Carlos, who was turning a big rack of ribs on the gas grill. He raised his tongs in greeting before turning his attention back to the food. "You guys want a drink?"

"Oh, yeah, that'd be great," Stevie said. "I can mix them, just show me where the stuff is."

"Right over there," Shawna said, nodding toward a table next to the wall of the building. "Help yourselves."

"Thanks, Shawna." Stevie grabbed Dan's hand and pulled him toward the drink table.

He could feel Dan's eyes on him while he filled two plastic cups with ice and whiskey and a splash of soda. He knew he looked hot. He'd worn the snug, low-riding black jeans and deep-purple shirt just for Dan. He'd bought the outfit on their last shopping trip, chiefly because of the way Dan's eyes had smoldered when he'd tried it on.

He lived for the fire he could call up in Dan's eyes sometimes. It hurt to know that he could never have anything more than that, but it was a pain he sought out constantly. Lately, he'd even started to see Dan's face instead of Jesse's when he and Jesse were in bed together. He'd close his eyes and imagine it was Dan's hands on his skin, Dan's kisses branding his body, Dan filling him up and bringing him to the brink.

"Hey, what's going on in there?"

Stevie shook himself and smiled up at Dan as he handed him his drink. "In where?"

Dan tapped the side of Stevie's head with one finger. "There. You looked awfully serious just now."

Stevie stared into Dan's dark eyes, and God, he wanted to tell him. Wanted to just say it, finally, just let out all the pent-up longing and tell Dan everything he felt for him. He licked his lips, watched Dan watching his mouth as he did it.

"Dan?" Stevie began. "I want ... I mean, I've been thinking ..."

He stopped, terrified suddenly. Pictures surfaced in his mind, snapshots of all the times he'd touched Dan, flirted and come on to him. All the times Dan had gently but firmly pushed him away. *Don't be an idiot, Sunshine*, he told himself. *He might be attracted, but he's not interested, and who could blame him? Just stop making an ass of yourself already.*

"What?" Dan stepped closer and bent down a little, curling one big hand around Stevie's arm. "You know you can talk to me, right? I won't tell anybody anything you don't want me to."

To his horror, Stevie felt his eyes begin to sting. He hung his head, letting his hair cover his eyes so Dan wouldn't see. "I know, Dan. But it's nothing, really. I just ... I've been thinking, you know, I've been working for a while now, and I think I've about got enough saved that I could find my own place soon. That's all."

Dan was silent. Stevie could hear him breathing. "You want to move out?"

No, Stevie thought, *I want to stay with you forever; I never want to leave, please keep me, please.* But he knew he couldn't say it.

"I'll never forget everything you've done for me, Dan," he said instead, eyes fixed on the ground at his feet. "You've been way better to me than I deserve. That's why I think I should move out. Because you've done enough. I can make my own way now, and it's time I did that and stopped taking advantage of you."

"Stevie, look at me," Dan said. Stevie reluctantly lifted his face. Dan's eyes were surprisingly sad.

"You don't have to leave if you don't want to." Dan's voice was so soft Stevie could barely hear him over the music and the growing crowd. "And you're sure as hell not taking advantage of me. I like having you around. But I understand why you'd want to have your own place." His eyes hardened. "You and Jesse ..."

"Yeah, you know what, let's not talk about him," Stevie interrupted. He flushed a little at the look in Dan's eyes.

"Where is he, anyhow?" Dan wandered away from the drinks table, making room for the growing numbers of people trying to get at the booze.

"He had to work." Stevie took a sip of his drink as he followed Dan across the yard. He didn't say so, but he was glad Jesse wasn't there.

"Hey, *amigos!*" Carlos called as they approached the grill. "How's things at the bookstore, Stevie?"

"Great. John and Evan should be here pretty soon. They're leaving the new girl to close up." Stevie reached out and swiped a finger full of spicy sauce off the ribs Carlos was grilling.

"Hey, hands off, bro!" Carlos smacked Stevie's hand with the tongs, getting more sauce on him. "So they hired someone else, huh?"

"Yeah. Her name's Megan. Nice girl." Stevie licked the barbeque sauce off his hand, knowing Dan was watching. "She's studying biology at UNCA, so she's only working part time, but it's been a big help. Especially for John. He actually gets a little time away from the register now."

"So when're those ribs gonna be done, Carlos?" Dan asked. "I'm starving for some meat." His dark eyes met Stevie's, thick and heavy, and Stevie nearly choked on his drink.

Carlos raised his eyebrows at them both. "Be ready in a few minutes, bro. Go on and dig into the other stuff though. There's some hot dogs over there someplace. Made 'em for the kids, but I think you could use one." He flashed an evil grin, and Dan blushed, dark eyes darting to Stevie's face.

Stevie and Dan stared at each other. Stevie felt like he was falling into those liquid eyes. He took a long swallow of whiskey and soda, licking the sharp, smoky taste off his lips. Dan's eyes followed the movement of his tongue.

"Stevie! Hi, sugar!"

Stevie blinked and turned toward John's voice. John waved at him and hurried toward them, dragging Evan behind him.

"Hi, guys," Dan said as John and Evan walked up. "Good to see you both. Um, I think I'm gonna get some of Shawna's cooking now. See you."

John stared at Dan's retreating back with raised eyebrows. "What got into him?"

"Nothing, that's the problem," Carlos muttered. Stevie stared at him in open-mouthed surprise. He grinned and winked. "So, guys, you have to meet my wife! Stevie, I can't leave the grill, man, will you get her for me?"

Stevie gave Carlos a narrow look. He smiled back, blandly innocent. Stevie shook his head. "Yeah, sure."

Stevie weaved through the crowd, speaking to various people as he slowly made his way over to the food table where Shawna stood talking to Dan. Which he strongly suspected was why Carlos had asked him to go find her.

"Sneaky bastard," Stevie muttered under his breath.

He could feel Dan watching him as he approached. He smiled brightly, trying to ignore the growing ache in his groin. "Hey, Shawna." He slung an arm around her shoulders. "Carlos wants you to come meet John and Evan, they're here."

"Oh, cool!" Shawna turned and kissed his cheek. "Thanks, hon. See you guys later." She squeezed Dan's hand and hurried off.

Stevie tossed back the rest of his drink and gave Dan his best Sunshine smile. "So what's good? I'm hungry."

"It's all good. Try any of it, you can't go wrong." Dan popped a baby carrot into his mouth and crunched noisily.

"Okay, let's see." Stevie considered the feast spread out on the table. "What's in the crock pot?"

"Those little sausage things."

"Oh, man, I love those."

"Then you have to try these, Shawna makes her own sauce. Extra spicy. You want another drink?"

"Sure."

Dan took Stevie's cup. "Coming right up."

When Dan got back a couple of minutes later, Stevie had piled a plate with sausages, fruit salad, and squares of pepper jack cheese. Dan laughed as he handed Stevie his drink.

"Interesting dinner, Stevie."

"Hey, what's the point of a party if you can't at least eat what you want?"

"Good point. C'mon, let's go sit down."

Dan picked up his plate and drink and headed toward the big, freestanding swing in the corner of the yard. Stevie followed him, enjoying the view. The sight of Dan's muscled ass in those well-worn jeans made his balls tighten. He figured it was a good thing his hands were full, because he didn't think he'd be able to resist a grope if he had one free.

They sat down together in the swing. Stevie pushed with his foot, setting it swaying gently. He set his drink down on the wooden arm of the swing's frame and picked up a small cocktail sausage.

"This is so cool." Stevie slid the sausage between his lips, sucking the sauce off.

"Yeah," Dan agreed absently, eyes glued to Stevie's mouth. "Um, what is?"

"The party." Stevie ran his tongue around one end of the sausage, watching Dan's eyes. "You okay, Dan?"

"S-sure. Um, yeah, fine." Dan picked up his drink and downed most of it in one gulp.

Stevie watched Dan's tongue flicker over his lips. It took everything he had to keep himself from tossing food and drink aside, throwing himself into Dan's arms, and having him right there in the swing. He sucked the sausage into his mouth, chewed and swallowed, did the same with another one. Dan watched his mouth the whole time.

It was the longest, most agonizingly sexual meal of Stevie's life. The fact that they both knew exactly what they were doing and were both pretending they didn't just added to the tension. Stevie nearly came in his pants when Dan slid one of the ribs he'd finally gotten into his mouth and sucked it clean.

By the time they'd gotten their fill of food, the party was in full swing. All the kids were upstairs in Carlos and Shawna's apartment, watching SpongeBob DVDs with the babysitter Shawna had hired for the evening. Carlos had put a mix CD on the player he'd attached to the outdoor speakers, and the yard seethed with people dancing. Stevie watched them with a smile.

"Hey, Dan," he said. "Want to dance?"

Dan grinned at him. "Stevie, you don't want to dance with me. I suck at it."

Stevie bit his tongue and didn't say what popped into his head. "Oh, c'mon, please? I wanna dance!" He hopped to his feet, swaying a little from the four stiff drinks he'd had, grabbed Dan's hands and pulled. "Come on, c'mon, c'mon!"

"No way," Dan laughed. "I've got two left feet anyhow, and I'm a little drunk right now."

"Fine, be that way." Stevie leaned close, letting his hair brush Dan's face, and smiled when Dan's breath ran out in a barely audible groan. "But you don't know what you're missing."

He pushed away, turned and walked off, smiling to himself. He knew he was just letting himself in for disappointment later, but right then he didn't care. All he cared about at that moment was the heat of Dan's gaze, practically burning the clothes off his back.

"Hey, John!" he called, spotting his friend talking to several other people a few feet away.

John turned, saw him and grinned. "Hi, sweetie!"

"I wanna dance, and Dan won't dance with me." Stevie grabbed John's wrist and tugged. "Come on, huh?"

John laughed. "Oh, I know just what you mean. Evan doesn't dance either, the big caveman. Not unless it's a slow dance, and that's only so he can grope my ass." He slipped his arm through Stevie's elbow. "Let's go, honey."

John was a perfect dance partner, matching Stevie step for step. After a few minutes, it got to be a competition to see who could invent the filthiest moves. By the time Placebo's cover of "I Feel You" ended, they were pressed tightly together, back to chest, Stevie grinding his ass against John's groin and John's hand sliding down the inside of Stevie's thigh. Both of them were giggling like crazy. Stevie couldn't remember when he'd had so much fun.

Evan, who'd been watching with evident amusement, cut in the minute a slow song came on. Stevie went to sit down next to Dan, who was still parked in the swing, practically invisible in the dense darkness under the big oak tree.

"Oh, man," he panted, wiping sweat off his brow. "That was awesome."

"I could tell." Dan grinned at him. "Put on quite a show there."

Stevie laughed. "John's crazy. That's why we get along so well."

"How come Evan doesn't get jealous?"

"Because he knows it's nothing but a little fun. He knows he's the only one John wants. I mean, look at 'em." Stevie nodded toward Evan and John, swaying to the music with their arms around each other. John's head rested on Evan's shoulder, Evan's hands caressed John's back. "They're nuts about each other. Crazy in love."

Dan nodded thoughtfully. "How long have they been together?"

"Twenty years, almost. Their anniversary's coming up in a couple of months."

"Wow. That's something."

"Yeah."

Silence. Stevie gazed out at the couples in the yard: John and Evan, Carlos and Shawna, Melina and the tall, model-handsome man Shawna had hooked her up with just a couple of weeks before. Several others, some of whom he recognized and some he didn't. They all seemed so happy, practically glowing with contentment. He wondered if he'd ever have that.

"Wonder what it's like?" Dan asked softly.

Stevie glanced at him. "What?"

"Being that much in love. Like Carlos and Shawna. Or John and Evan."

"Dan, I swear you must be psychic, 'cause I was just thinking the same thing."

Dan was silent for a moment, watching the couples dancing. Then he turned to face Stevie, pulling one foot up to rest on the seat of the swing. "Stevie, can I ask you something?"

Stevie looked hard at Dan, trying to read his face. His dark eyes gleamed in the dimness, flickering with a faint orange light from the torches Carlos had lit in the yard, but his expression was unreadable.

"Sure, Dan." Stevie folded one leg underneath him and inched closer. "What is it?"

Dan leaned forward, brows drawing together. "I hope I'm not being too nosy here, but how do you feel about Jesse? Do you love him?" Dan bit his lip, sending a shiver of need through Stevie's bones. "Because I don't think you do."

Stevie shook his head. "No. I don't love him."

"Then why do you keep seeing him? I'm sorry, Stevie, but I just don't get it, and it's been bugging me."

"Why?"

"Because ..." Dan stopped and hung his head, inspecting his fingernails. "I just think you can do better, that's all. That boy doesn't care about you, Stevie. You're just another thing to him, just something else he can say is his." He raised his head again, and the intensity of his gaze turned Stevie's legs to rubber. "You deserve more than that."

Stevie stared, stunned. The way Dan was looking at him ... was it more than lust, or was that just wishful thinking? He didn't know, didn't trust himself to figure it out. He licked his lips and made himself say something, anything, before he threw good sense out the window and himself into Dan's arms.

"Oh, yeah, I mean, I know he doesn't care anything about me, and maybe, maybe he's using me -- hell, I know he is -- but I'm using him, too, you know, I mean he, he's pretty damn good between the sheets, right, and he's not ... you know ... a customer ... and I, I needed that, right ... it feels good to have somebody touch me without paying for it, and ... and ..."

Dan's fingers against his lips dried the words in Stevie's throat. He stared up into Dan's eyes, willing him to understand.

Dan smiled gently, moving his hand away from Stevie's mouth to push the sweaty tangles out of his eyes. "You're babbling."

Stevie laughed nervously. "Yeah, well. Sorry."

"Don't be sorry." Dan slid closer, until their knees bumped. "Hey, Stevie?"

"Yeah, Dan?"

Silence, thick and charged. Dan's big hand cupped Stevie's cheek, thumb rubbing his lower lip. Stevie's skin felt electrified, every nerve raw and jumping. Dan leaned down toward him, and Stevie realized what he was doing a split second before their lips met.

For a heartbeat, Stevie was paralyzed. Then all his careful defenses crumbled like ash when Dan's tongue slid over his lips, urging them apart. He opened gladly, tilting his head and burying both hands in Dan's thick, dark hair. The feel of Dan's tongue against his turned him liquid with desire.

"Dan. Oh." Stevie rose up on his knees, cradling Dan's face in his hands, licking at his lips. "Want you so bad. I've wanted you for so long."

"God, Stevie." Dan pulled back a little, stroking Stevie's hair and staring into his eyes. "Stevie, I ..."

A sudden crash startled them apart. Stevie turned around just in time to see Carlos trotting toward them, chasing the football that had just come hurtling through the branches above their heads.

"Sorry," Carlos panted. "Evan throws really hard, you know?" He scooped up the football, flashed them a grin, and jogged off again.

Stevie stared after him, trying to catch his breath. The music had changed, and there seemed to be an impromptu game of touch football going on. How long had he and Dan been kissing, anyway? It didn't feel like nearly long enough to Stevie. He turned to Dan, reaching for him, already addicted to the soaring rush of Dan's mouth on his. When he saw Dan's face, though, his happy smile faded.

"Dan?" He reached out and touched Dan's cheek, tentative now. "What's wrong?"

Dan stared at him, dark eyes huge and shocked. His hands shook as he pushed Stevie away. "I ... shit. Stevie, we ... oh, God ... I'm sorry, I ... I can't ..." He stood, gave Stevie a look full of need and confusion and fear, then turned and strode off toward the back door.

Stevie sat there, feeling like his guts had been ripped right out of him. He couldn't move, couldn't speak, couldn't even think. For a few shining minutes, he'd had everything he'd ever wanted. Been happier than he could ever remember feeling in his life. And then he saw the horror on Dan's face when he realized what he'd just done.

Should've known it couldn't be real, he thought. *He knows what you are, and it couldn't ever be real.* Hot tears pricked his eyelids, and he blinked them away. *What do you have to cry about, Sunshine, huh?* he asked himself. *You did this to yourself, now fucking deal with it.* He sniffed deeply and scrubbed the tears off his cheeks.

"Stevie? I saw Dan running off, he looked like ... Oh. Oh, honey, what's the matter?"

Stevie looked up at John, knowing he looked as devastated as he felt and trying like hell not to. "Nothing, John, I'm fine."

John dismissed the obvious lie with a wave of his hand. "Honey, you can't fool me with that fake smile of yours." He sat down on the swing and took Stevie's hand firmly in both of his. "Now you just tell Uncle Johnny all about it."

Stevie tried to lie, tried to smile and laugh and hide his hurt like he always did. But he couldn't. He was tired. So tired of pretending everything was all right when it wasn't. He drew a deep, shuddering breath.

"He kissed me, John. You know how long I've wanted that?" He shook his head. "I've been in love with him since day one. And it felt so fucking good for him to kiss me like that. Don't think I've ever been so happy."

John laced his fingers through Stevie's, squeezing his hand. "And then?"

"And then, he just ... just said he couldn't, then ran away." Stevie leaned his head against John's shoulder.

"Why do you think he ran away, sweetie?"

Stevie sighed. "He doesn't want me, John."

John laughed. "Honey, that's crap, and you know it. That man needs a bib when he's around you, he drools so much."

"Yeah, I know he's attracted to me. But he doesn't want to be with me."

"Baby, what on earth makes you think that?"

Stevie chewed his lip, thinking hard. He wanted to tell John, but didn't think he could stand it if it cost him his job at Rainbow Books. He lifted his head and stared hard into John's kind eyes.

"I've done some pretty bad things, John," he said. His voice sounded small and afraid in his own ears.

"What could you possibly have done that's so terrible? Do you torture kittens in your spare time?"

Stevie laughed in spite of himself, and John grinned at him. "It's not like that. But it's bad enough. I can't blame him. He could sure as hell do better."

John studied Stevie's face with unusual seriousness. "Honey, I know you don't want to tell me why you think you're not good enough. I wish you would, but I won't push you. But I don't need to know your deep, dark secrets to know that you're wrong about Dan."

Stevie shook his head. "No, I'm not. Every time I touch him, he pushes me away. He just doesn't want me, John."

"Yes, he does. And I'm not just talking about sex here. He's obviously got the hot pants for you, but it's more than that. I think Dan has serious feelings for you."

"Then why does he push me away all the time, huh?" Stevie's eyes welled up and spilled over. John wiped the tears off his cheeks.

"He's scared, honey." John's voice was soft and gentle. "He's been in the closet his whole life, and he's scared of coming out and risking everything he cares about."

Stevie stared silently at John. "But ... but he's got to know that no one's gonna care. They won't stop loving him just because he's gay."

"We know that, sweetie, but it's not so easy when you're the one with so much to lose if you're wrong." John smiled, a little sadly this time. "I thought my parents would accept my being gay. But I was wrong. They haven't spoken to me since the day I told them, nearly thirty years ago."

"Jesus, John." Stevie squeezed John's hand. "That's awful."

"It was at first, it really was. Still hurts sometimes. But I learned to accept it. And when Evan came along ..." John stopped, his eyes going shiny and far away. "Well. I don't need anything else, as long as I have him." His eyes focused on Stevie again. "But that's why Dan's afraid, honey. Because no matter how well you think you know someone, you never really know them until you tell them you aren't the person they always thought you were. That's when you find out who you can count on and who you can't."

Stevie was silent for a moment. "I think I understand. But John, I think they already know. Carlos and Shawna, I'm pretty sure they know. They just don't want to say anything because they're waiting for him."

"Give him a little time, honey. I think he'll come around." John patted Stevie's cheek. "And you need to stop thinking you're not good enough for him. Whatever it is you've done, sweetie, Dan doesn't care. He's got it bad for you. He just needs to decide for himself that you're more important to him than keeping his secret."

Stevie smiled through the tears that refused to stop. "I guess so. Thanks, John. You're the best." He threw both arms around John's neck and hugged him hard.

"Glad I can help, sweetie." John pulled back, brushed more tears off of Stevie's cheek. "You know, it may be best for both of you if you weren't living together."

Stevie nodded. "Yeah, I think you're right. I was thinking of moving out anyway, because I feel like I've sponged off of Dan for too long as it is. But now ... Hell, I don't know if I can even look him in the eye anymore, never mind live with him." He laughed bitterly. "I sure as fuck can't walk around the place naked anymore."

John clucked his tongue. "Well, no wonder he can't get himself straightened out! Who the hell could, with such fineness strutting around all bare and tempting?"

Stevie laughed. "Keep talking, John, and you'll talk me right out of my mood."

"That's the idea, sugar. Listen, you can come stay with Evan and me if you want. That way you can go ahead and get out right away, and it'll give you and Dan both time to think."

"Oh, John, I couldn't do that. I don't want to just sponge off you guys instead."

"You wouldn't be. We have a detached garage with a little apartment above it. It's tee-tiny, but clean and cozy and just cute as hell. You could rent it. We've been talking about renting it out anyhow, and it'd be so much better to have someone we know there rather than a stranger."

Stevie sat in stunned silence for a moment. Then a big grin spread over his face. "That'd be great, John, thanks! You sure Evan won't mind?"

"Won't mind what?"

Stevie turned to see Evan strolling up to them, smiling, dark eyes twinkling. "What's he trying to talk you into, Stevie? Be careful, he's full of nefarious plans."

"The only nefarious plans I have are for your sweet ass, smarty." John jumped up and wound his arms around Evan's waist. "Stevie's looking for his own place, and I was just telling him he could rent the apartment over the garage."

"Good idea." Evan tilted John's face up and kissed him, then turned to smile at Stevie. "You can move in any time, Stevie, it's furnished and everything."

Stevie leapt to his feet, flung himself at John and Evan, and hugged them both until they gasped for breath. "You guys are the best friends anybody could have. Thank you, I mean it."

"You're a good kid, Stevie," Evan said. "You just let us know when you want to move in, we'll help you move."

"I don't have much," Stevie said. "Just clothes and CDs and a few books. All I need is a ride."

"You got it, honey," John said. "What about tomorrow? Take the morning off; then call me when you wake up, and I'll come get you."

"That'd be great, John, thanks." Stevie smiled. "You guys are so good to me."

John pulled him into a hug. "We love you, sweetie." He patted Stevie's back, then turned to whisper in his ear. "You hang in there, okay? Dan's a smart boy; he won't let you get away."

Stevie sat back down in the swing as John and Evan said good-night and headed, hand in hand, to the front parking lot and home. He sat and cried silently until the tears trickled to a halt. Then he plastered on his brightest smile and went to face the world again.

* * * * *

He stayed until all the other guests left, nibbling and drinking and making small talk, slipping into his Sunshine skin like a pair of well-worn slippers. Hiding the deep ache inside him behind flirting words and a brilliant smile. After the last guests said their good-byes, he stayed and helped Shawna and Carlos put away the leftover food and pick up the trash. They both kept giving him concerned looks, but neither said anything. He was grateful for that.

Finally, though, the yard was clean, and Carlos and Shawna had hugged him good-night and gone to their apartment, and he didn't have any excuses left. He stood in front of Dan's door for five solid minutes before he worked up the courage to open it. Dan had left it unlocked, thank God. He hadn't brought his key to the party. Hadn't thought he'd need it. Wouldn't need it anymore, after tomorrow. The thought hurt something deep and vital in him.

He stopped at the open door to Dan's bedroom, unable to help himself. He could just make out Dan's bulk in the bed, curled up on his side, his back to the door. Faint golden light from the walkway outside bled through the blinds to gild Dan's bare shoulder. The sight of that smooth skin, which he wanted to touch so badly and couldn't, brought the tears again. He wiped them away.

"God, Dan," he whispered. "I love you so much. I wish I was good enough for you."

He turned away before the leaking sadness could become full-blown sobs. He brushed his teeth, stripped off his clothes, and started to curl up naked on the couch like he usually did. Then he stopped. He found a pair of shorts and pulled them on, then lay down and pulled the blanket up to his chin.

The sky outside had begun to gray by the time exhaustion finally tugged his eyes closed.

CHAPTER NINE

It was after ten when Dan woke up Saturday morning. He lay staring at the ceiling, thinking about the night before.

About Stevie.

Stevie's mouth, silky soft, warm and wet and alive under his. Just thinking of that kiss made him burn.

The memory of the look on Stevie's face when he ran away quenched the fire like a bucket of ice water.

Dan sat up and buried his face in his hands. It made him sick to know how badly he'd hurt Stevie by what he'd done. And there was no doubt that he'd hurt him. Dan thought he'd never stop seeing the raw pain in those sky-blue eyes when he pushed Stevie away.

He still wasn't sure exactly why he'd done it. Kissing Stevie felt so good, so completely natural. He'd acted on instinct, finally giving in to the desires he'd bottled up for so long, and it had felt utterly right. But when Carlos showed up, chasing that damn football, all his fears had come rushing back. Fear of discovery, of his lies being found out. Fear of stripping away all the lifelong deceptions and revealing his true self to the world. He'd panicked and run away.

"Dan, you damn jackass," he muttered to himself. "You're gonna have to fix this."

The thought of facing Stevie now made his guts twist with dread. It was the possibility of what could happen if he just overcame his fear and told Stevie how he felt that pushed him to his feet and out the bedroom door.

Stevie lay curled on the sofa, still deeply asleep, the blanket clutched tightly around him. He looked tired. Skin too pale, dark circles under his eyes, and eyelids that looked pink and puffy. Dan stood there, chewing his thumb, torn between letting Stevie sleep and waking him so he could apologize before he lost his nerve. Eventually he headed into the kitchen and started making coffee, vowing to talk to Stevie as soon as he woke up.

He was in the bedroom, sipping his second cup while he dressed, when he heard Stevie stir in the living room. He closed his eyes and took several deep breaths, trying to calm his racing heart. It was several minutes before he could work up the courage to leave his bedroom again.

His carefully thought out apology went right out the window when he saw Stevie taking his clothes out of the built-in storage under the window seat and piling them into a big plastic bag, along with his CDs, some magazines, and a few books. Dan stared, heart thumping.

"Stevie? What're you doing?"

Stevie finished folding a t-shirt, turned and looked at Dan. His eyes were red and swollen and heartbroken. It killed Dan to see Stevie trying to hide behind his automatic smile when the sadness in his eyes was too big to disguise.

"John and Evan are going to let me rent the apartment over their garage. I called John, he'll be over in a few minutes to pick me up."

Dan blinked. "You're really moving out? Why?"

"Come on, Dan. You don't have to pretend you want me to stay. It's okay, really, I totally understand."

"Stevie, no, you don't have to ..."

"Just stop it." Stevie threw down the jeans he'd been folding and wrapped both arms around himself. "You don't have to feel bad, Dan. We both need some time here, right? You need to ... to figure out what it is you want. And I need to be away from you while you do that." He raised his wounded eyes to Dan's face. "I just can't do this anymore. I can't stay here when I lo-- when I want you so bad and I never know when you're gonna want me, too, or when you're gonna reject me. It's just too fucking hard."

Dan swallowed. "I ... I'm sorry. I've wanted you since the first time I saw you. But I'm scared, Stevie. I don't know why, it's just ... Hell. It changes everything, and to tell you the truth, I don't know if I can handle that right now. I don't know if I can handle telling everybody the truth after all this time."

Stevie nodded, his face more serious than Dan had ever seen it. "I know. This is the best thing for both of us." The corners of his mouth lifted in a tiny smile. "No matter what happens between us, Dan, you saved me. You gave me the chance to start over, and I won't forget that. So no hard feelings, huh?"

Dan shook his head. His throat felt raw and tight. "Not on my end. And it's more than I deserve if you don't hate me right now."

The doorbell rang. They both glanced at the door, then back at each other. Dan wanted more than anything to beg Stevie to stay, to promise him the world and everything in it if only he wouldn't leave. But Dan couldn't be sure he wouldn't react the same way again, and that wouldn't be fair to Stevie. So he bit his tongue and made himself keep quiet. Stevie grabbed his bags, then turned back to Dan.

"I couldn't ever hate you." Stevie's voice shook with suppressed emotion. The blue of his eyes shone bright and intense against the redness. He held out a hand. Dan shook it, feeling numb and a little unreal. "Take care of yourself, Dan. I ..." Stevie bit his lip, brushed past Dan and strode out the door.

Dan caught a glimpse of John's worried expression before the door slammed shut. He sat down on the sofa and stared at the wall, wondering if he'd ever stop feeling so torn.

* * * * *

Dan had known he'd miss Stevie. But he hadn't counted on the vastness of Stevie's absence, or the barbed pain that tugged at his guts every morning when he woke up and remembered. He still saw Stevie from time to time, usually when Dan gave in to his longing and visited the bookstore. But the brief words they exchanged, the polite smiles, only made him hurt more. And watching Stevie with Jesse, when he knew there was nothing real between them, was pure agony. Especially since he knew in his heart what he and Stevie could have together, if he could only stop being such a damn coward.

During the first few days after Stevie moved out, Dan almost went to him any number of times. He wanted more than anything to take Stevie into his arms, hold him and kiss him and tell him ...

But he couldn't say it, not even to himself. And he didn't want to cause Stevie any more pain. So he stayed away, and kept the feelings he couldn't express deep inside.

The days stretched into three of the longest weeks Dan could ever remember. He tried to pretend that nothing had changed and that he was doing fine. But he wasn't nearly as good an actor as he thought, or so he learned when Melina showed up at his apartment on a chilly Friday evening in mid-October.

"I've been calling you for four days!" Melina exclaimed as soon as Dan opened the door after she rang the bell for the second time. "What's going on?"

"C'mon in, Melina." Dan stood aside and held the door open. "Sorry. Guess I've been a little busy lately."

"Yeah, busy moping." Melina dropped her purse on the table and curled up in the big armchair. Dan started to sit down, too, and she held a hand out. "Uh-uh. Go get dressed. I'm taking you out."

Dan sighed and rubbed his eyes. "Thanks anyhow, but I really don't much feel like going out, if it's all the same to you."

"It isn't." She narrowed her eyes and pointed a bright green-painted fingernail at him. "You've been sulking in this damn apartment for too long. You're putting on something that shows off that hot bod, and we're going out."

"I haven't been sulking."

"Yeah, you have. And if you're not going to fight for Stevie, then you have to get on with your life." She jumped up, turned Dan around, and gave him a push before he could say a thing. "Now go on, get dressed. We're meeting Carlos and Shawna at Barley's in half an hour."

Dan trudged obediently into the bedroom and started changing from the sweats he'd put on after his shower into a pair of body hugging jeans and a dark blue sweater. He dreaded even leaving his apartment anymore, but he knew Melina was right. He was in serious danger of becoming a hermit if he didn't get out once in a while.

"Okay, I'm ready," Dan said as he emerged from the bedroom. He spread his arms and did a slow turn. "Good enough?"

Melina grinned. "Dan, you are beyond fine."

"Thanks," Dan said, laughing. "Looking pretty hot yourself there, lady. Hey, you still seeing that guy Shawna fixed you up with? What's his name?"

"Aaron. Yeah, he's taking me to some formal party or other tomorrow night. Some kind of charity thing, I forget what exactly." She smiled, green eyes shining. "He's great. I can't believe Shawna finally found me Mr. Right."

"No kidding." Dan scooped his keys off the table, found his wallet, and shoved both into his jeans pockets.

"Why don't you tell them, Dan? Carlos and Shawna, I mean. Do you really think they don't know, or at least suspect?"

Dan locked the apartment door, and they headed for the stairs to the parking lot. "I guess they probably figured it out a long time ago."

"Then why don't you just tell them and get it over with?"

Dan thought about that. He'd been thinking about it a lot lately. And try as he might, he could no longer think of a single reason not to come clean. Years of keeping secrets had only ended up causing pain, not only to himself, but to Stevie.

"You're right, Melina," Dan said finally. He took a deep breath. "I'm gonna tell them. And I may as well do it now. Tonight."

"Good." Melina unlocked her car, and they climbed in. "You're doing the right thing, Dan."

Dan gave her a weak smile. "I sure as hell hope so."

* * * * *

Barley's was packed to the rafters. The big, wood-paneled room rang with laughter, bluegrass music, and the clink of glasses. Carlos and Shawna were already there. Dan and Melina made their way through the crowd to the corner table where Carlos stood waving at them.

"*Hola*," Carlos said as they all sat down. "Wow, you actually got him out of the apartment, Melina! You da man!"

Melina laughed. "Wasn't easy, let me tell you."

"I bet," Shawna said. She reached across the table and squeezed Dan's hand. "How're you doing, Dan? I haven't seen you in a long time."

Dan smiled at her. "I'm doing okay. Been busy."

"Yeah, busy. Whatever you say, bro." Carlos raised a skeptical eyebrow.

Dan flushed. "Um, guys? I want to ... to tell you something. And I need to do it right now, before I lose my nerve."

Carlos and Shawna glanced at each other, then turned identical eager expressions to Dan. "What is it, Dan?" Shawna asked.

Dan took a deep breath, let it out slowly. "Okay, here goes." He reached for Melina's hand. She laced her fingers through his and squeezed, and he gave her a grateful smile. "Guys, I'm ... uh ... I'm ..." He fell silent, staring at the table.

"Say it, *hermano*," Carlos said, his voice soft and much more serious than usual. "It's okay."

"Yeah. I guess it is, huh?" Dan smiled. "Guys, I'm gay."

Shawna let out a long breath. "Well, it's about time you told us. I was getting tired of setting you up with women and telling them you're super picky and not to expect anything."

Carlos laughed. "Yeah, it didn't take us long to figure out why you never were interested in the girls she set you up with. I told her she should quit, but you know how stubborn she is. Said one day you'd get sick of it and admit that you're gay." He grinned at his wife. "Told you it wouldn't work, babe."

"Shut up, Carlos," she said, nudging her husband's shoulder. "Here's the beer."

The waitress smiled as she set a mug down in front of each of them. "Y'all ready to order?"

"Few more minutes?" Melina said. "We haven't really looked at the menu yet."

"Sure thing," the waitress said. "Be back in a little bit."

She turned away and hurried off to the next table. Carlos waited until she was out of earshot, then leaned over the table toward Dan.

"So now that you're not trying to keep it a secret," he said, "you gonna go make up with Stevie, or what? I mean I don't know exactly what happened, but something sure as shit did."

Dan took a long swallow of beer. He could feel his cheeks reddening with embarrassment. *Stop being so stupid*, he scolded himself. *They know now -- hell, they always knew -- and they don't care. They're your friends, you can talk to them.*

"I don't know," he answered finally. "I mean, I want to. But he's still with Jesse, isn't he?" He stopped, shaking his head. "I hurt him bad. What if he doesn't want anything to do with me now? Not that I'd blame him."

"Well, he and Jesse are still seeing each other," Melina said thoughtfully, "but it doesn't seem to be anything serious. I know for a fact that Jesse goes out with other guys sometimes. I'm pretty sure Stevie knows it, too." She shrugged. "To tell you the truth, I don't think either one of them would be sorry to break up. I'm not even sure why they're still together. Guess it's just gotten comfortable or something."

"Probably," Shawna said. "I've done that before. My high school boyfriend and I went out for over two years, but we weren't ever that crazy about each other. It was just fun, you know? Just sort of an automatic date for the weekends. Carlos is the first and only guy I've ever been in love with." She leaned her head on Carlos's shoulder and smiled up at him.

"*Te amo*," Carlos murmured, nuzzling Shawna's hair.

"Love you, too, honey." Shawna raised her face, and they kissed.

Dan watched, smiling to himself. He imagined being with Stevie like that, crazy in love and completely gone on each other. And for the first time, he truly believed that it might happen.

* * * * *

Dan tried to wait, at least until the next day. But now that he'd formally outed himself, his feelings for Stevie solidified, sharpened, and prodded him into calling Stevie's apartment as soon as he got home. Melina gladly gave him the number, which she'd gotten from Jesse soon after Stevie moved.

"I was sort of hoping you'd call him before this," she said. "But hey, as long as you're finally making a move, I'm not complaining."

"Thanks, Melina. I mean that. You've been great to me." Dan hugged her, then got out of the car and leaned down to peer inside. "You sure Jesse's not gonna be pissed off? Or Stevie?"

"I can't be totally sure about anything, Dan. Jesse has a nasty temper sometimes. But I'm sure they're not serious about each other. And I'm pretty sure Stevie would drop Jesse like a bad habit if he thought he had a chance with you. And I know for a fact how you feel about him. So go for it."

"Okay. Yeah, I'm gonna call him soon as I get upstairs."

"Great. And let me know what happens, huh?"

"Sure thing. 'Night, Melina. And thanks."

Melina smiled. "'Night, Dan. Good luck."

Dan shut the door. Melina drove off, and he headed up the steps to his apartment. Inside, he sat and stared at the phone for several minutes, trying to work up the courage to dial Stevie's number.

"Just do it, dumbass," he ordered himself. He nodded, picked the phone up and dialed before he could change his mind.

Stevie answered on the first ring. "'Lo?"

Dan swallowed. "Uh. Hi. Hi, Stevie, it's ... it's Dan."

Silence on the other end. Then Stevie's voice, guarded and hesitant. "Hey."

"Hey. Um, listen, are you busy right now?"

"No, not really. Just watching TV."

"So ... Jesse's not there?"

"No. He's out. With some friends."

Dan figured he could guess what sort of "friends," from the exasperated tone of Stevie's voice as much as from what Melina had told him. "Oh. Okay." He fell silent again, his mind a blank all of a sudden.

"Dan? You okay?" Stevie sounded concerned. Worried about him. It made Dan's eyes sting.

"Yeah, I'm fine. But, listen, could I come over? I really need to talk to you."

Stevie was quiet for a moment, and a hard knot of dread formed in Dan's stomach. Maybe he'd waited too long, maybe Stevie was over whatever he'd once felt for Dan, maybe ...

"Okay, yeah. Come on over. You know where it is?"

Dan let out a sigh of relief. "No. Hang on, let me get a pencil."

Dan ran into the kitchen to get the pencil and notepad Stevie had always kept in there to write grocery lists on. He himself never used it, but he'd never been able to get rid of it after Stevie left. It made his pulse race with excitement to think of once again being able to walk into this room and see Stevie leaning on the counter, three-quarters naked and singing along with whatever CD was on, scribbling a grocery list while he cooked. He'd missed that.

Stevie gave him directions, and within fifteen minutes Dan was standing at the door of Stevie's apartment, heart thudding against his ribs. He wiped his palms on his jeans, took a deep breath, and knocked firmly on the door. It opened almost before he'd finished knocking, and Dan stood staring into those beautiful blue eyes that he'd missed so much.

"Hi, Dan." Stevie smiled and stood aside, holding the door open. "C'mon in."

"Thanks." Dan stepped inside and glanced around. The place was small, clean and bright, and surprisingly bare. A few plastic bags sat against the wall at the foot of the bed. "Looks like you haven't finished unpacking yet."

Stevie hung his head and peered up at Dan through a veil of hair. It had grown some, Dan thought. He stuck his hands in his pockets to keep himself from burying them in that shining gold.

"I've been working a lot. Haven't really had much time." Stevie bit his lip. "So. How've you been, Dan?"

"Good." He shook his head. "No, wait. That's a lie. I haven't been good at all. I've been hurting pretty bad."

Stevie stepped closer, brows drawing together in worry. "You have? What is it? Are you sick?"

"No, nothing like that. I just ... I've been thinking about that night. About ... about kissing you. And how good it felt, and how badly I treated you after. I wish I hadn't done that. Pushed you away, I mean."

"I've thought about it, too, Dan." Stevie's voice was so soft Dan could barely hear him. "I can't stop thinking about it."

Dan gulped and made himself go on. "I told Carlos and Shawna. Just now, just tonight. I told them I'm gay."

Stevie stared hard at him, blue eyes on fire. "So. So you're, like, out now? For real?"

"Yeah. No more secrets." Dan laughed. "Feels great to not be lying for a change." He took Stevie's hand in his. "I'm not scared anymore, Stevie. Don't know if that matters now or not, but I have to try."

Stevie blinked up at him. "Does ... does that mean ... what?"

Dan pulled Stevie closer, winding their fingers together. *Now or never, Danny-boy*, he told himself. *Take the goddamn plunge already. For once in your sorry life, don't take the easy way out.*

"It means," Dan said softly, "that I want to try with you. I think we could have something good." He caressed Stevie's cheek with his free hand. "I love you, Stevie."

Stevie went still, his gaze locked with Dan's. His fingers trembled in Dan's grip. "Even though I'm a whore?"

"That's all behind you. That's not who you are anymore. But I'd love you no matter what." Dan ran his fingertips down Stevie's cheek. "Stevie? Am I too late? It is too late for us?"

A wide smile spread across Stevie's face. "No, it's not too late. God, Dan. I've been in love with you ever since you came through that door and rescued me." He reached up and wound his arms around Dan's neck. "I love you, Dan. I love you so fucking much."

Dan smiled, cupped Stevie's head in his hand and bent to kiss him. Stevie's mouth opened with a soft sigh, tongue sliding against Dan's. His heart pounded fast and hard against Dan's chest. It felt like the most natural thing in the world to hold him close and taste that sweet mouth.

"What the fuck's going on?"

Jesse. Dan felt Stevie tense in his arms. He pulled away, but kept hold of Stevie's hand. Jesse stood in the open doorway, fists clenched, eyes sparking with anger.

"Jesse," Stevie said. "What're you doing here? I thought you were going out."

"I did go out," Jesse said. "Now I'm back." He didn't even glance at Dan, but kept his eyes fixed on Stevie.

Stevie flushed. Ignoring Jesse's murderous glare, he turned back to Dan. "Listen, Dan, why don't you head on home now, huh? I think I need to talk to Jesse."

Dan shot a worried look in Jesse's direction. "So ... so, what ..."

"We're okay, Dan. I need to explain to him, and I think it's better if I do that in private." Stevie stood on tiptoe to whisper in Dan's ear. "Everything's fine now."

Dan pulled Stevie close again and kissed him, taking perverse delight in doing it right in front of Jesse. "Call me later, okay? So I'll know you're all right." He shot a hurt-him-and-you're-dead look at Jesse, who paled a little but didn't say anything.

"Okay. 'Bye, Dan." Stevie smiled at him, almost stopping Dan's heart.

"'Bye. Talk to you later." Dan gave Stevie a smile full of promises, frowned fiercely at Jesse, and forced himself out the door.

He hummed to himself on the way down the stairs and out to his Jeep, feeling happier and more peaceful that he'd felt since ... well, ever, as far as he could remember. The future had suddenly become blindingly bright, and he wanted to shout it to the world.

He worried a little about Stevie being alone with Jesse. The expression on Jesse's face had said he got Dan's message loud and clear: hurt Stevie, and Dan hurts you. But he still worried. Though nothing could eclipse his happiness at that moment.

He turned up the radio and sang along as he pulled the Jeep out into the street.

CHAPTER TEN

Stevie watched Dan walk out the door and wished he could go with him. He wanted desperately to undress Dan and kiss every inch of that gorgeous, bronzed, work-hardened body. Later, he promised himself. He squared his shoulders and met Jesse's eyes.

"Jesse," he said, "we have to talk."

"No shit, Sherlock." Jesse crossed his arms and frowned even harder. "So talk. Fucking explain to me why the fuck I come in here and find you with your tongue down that fucking caveman's throat."

"First of all, his name is Dan. Second of all, you wouldn't have seen that if you ever bothered to knock."

"Maybe you should lock the door next time you're fucking around behind my back," Jesse sneered.

"Says the guy who just got done blowing some twink in the back seat of a '76 Nova," Stevie shot back.

Jesse's face darkened. "What?"

"You heard me. That's what your so-called 'friend' Devon drives, right? And you were out with him, and God knows who all else, and I know just what you were doing because you've done it so many times before. Hell, if I kissed you right now I bet you'd taste like ten different kinds of come. And then you have the fucking nerve to yell at me for kissing somebody else? We never said we were exclusive." Stevie shook his head. "Here I thought breaking up with you would be hard. I felt bad because I was afraid you'd be upset. Thanks for making it easy on me."

Jesse stood there, open-mouthed and shaking, for a long moment. Finally he stalked up to Stevie and pointed a finger in his face.

"You," he said, his voice low and venomous, "are mine. You hear me? Mine!"

Stevie clenched his teeth and counted to ten in his head. "Get out, Jesse. I don't want to see you again."

He brushed past Jesse, intending to open the door and send Jesse on his way. Jesse grabbed his arm and whirled him around, crushing their bodies together. "I don't think so."

Jesse snatched a handful of Stevie's hair and kissed him hard. Stevie bit Jesse's lip, and Jesse pulled back with a cry, blood dripping down his chin. He stared at Stevie with fury blazing in his eyes. Then before Stevie knew what was happening, Jesse's fist connected with his cheek. He staggered and fell, stunned by the blow. Jesse hauled him up again by the armpits.

"I said," Jesse growled, "that you are mine. Fucking little whore!"

For a heartbeat, Stevie's whole world went still and silent. Then a rage like he'd never felt in his life shot through him like a firestorm. He kicked Jesse in the knee and shoved him as hard as he could. Jesse went down. Stevie flung himself on top of him, knocking him flat on his back on the floor.

"I am not a whore!" Stevie screamed. "Don't you ever call me that, you fucking piece of shit!" He grabbed Jesse's hair in both hands and slammed his head against the floor. Jesse cried out in pain. "Dan loves me, and I love him, and I don't ever want to see you again! Now get the fuck out!"

Stevie let go and stood up, fists still clenched. Jesse pushed himself slowly to his feet. He regarded Stevie cautiously with round, shocked eyes.

"You're fucking crazy, man," he said, his voice higher than normal. Stevie could see the fear in his eyes.

"Go away, Jesse. Don't ever come near me again."

Jesse opened his mouth, closed it again, yanked the door open, and was gone. Stevie stumbled to the bed and sat down, shaking with reaction. It surprised him and scared him a little, to know that he was capable of such violence. He fervently hoped that Jesse would be the first and last person to inspire such a reaction, because he didn't like it at all. Rage that strong felt brutal and ugly, and he never wanted to feel it again.

The phone rang just as he got up to call Dan. He picked it up and smiled when he heard Dan's worried voice on the other end.

"Hi, Dan."

"Hey. You okay? I know you were gonna call me later, but I just ... I just got this feeling, and I was worried, so ..."

"I'm glad you called me." Stevie sat down on the bed. "It was pretty ugly."

"Did he hurt you? I swear, if he laid a finger on you, I'll kick his ass into next week." The anger was palpable in Dan's voice.

"Well, he kind of hit me. But," Stevie continued when he heard Dan sputtering with fury, "I got him good. He's probably scared of me now."

"Good, because I don't wanna go to jail for murder, and I'd sure as hell murder the bastard if he ever touches you again."

Stevie laughed. "It was worth it, then. I don't want you to go to jail either."

"So what'd you do to him?"

"I tackled him and banged his head on the floor. After he hit me. So he started it."

"Bastard."

"Don't think about him anymore, Dan. I'm sure as hell not going to."

"Deal." Dan's voice dropped down low. "Wish I was there with you, Stevie."

"Me, too. I miss you already."

"You want me to come over again?"

He did. Badly. "You don't have to do that, Dan, it's okay. I hate for you to drive all the way back here after you just got home."

"I don't mind. It's not far."

"Are you sure? I mean, I really, really want to be with you right now, but it just seems like such a pain for you to turn right around and come back here, you know?"

"It's not a pain, Stevie. It's nothing at all."

A knock sounded on the door. Stevie glared at it. "Hang on, someone's at the door."

He got up, crossed the room in a few strides, and opened the door, belatedly wondering if it was Jesse and what he'd do if it was.

It wasn't.

Dan stood on the other side of the door, cell phone pressed to his ear, grinning. "Hang up, Stevie, you got company."

Stevie clicked the phone off and set it on the little table beside the door. "Dan, what ... how ..."

"I never left." Dan shoved his cell phone into his jacket pocket. "I parked just past the house and waited for that little jackass to leave." He shrugged off his jacket, which dropped unnoticed to the floor, and gently touched Stevie's injured cheek. "That son of a bitch. I'm gonna kill him."

Stevie laughed. "Don't bother. He won't be bugging me anymore. He thinks I'm a nut job now."

Dan's hand slid around to the back of Stevie's neck, caressing, fingers twining in his hair. "Stevie. God, I want you so damn much right now."

"Oh. Dan. C'mere." Stevie reached a hand up and pulled Dan's face down to his.

The kiss was deep and urgent. Needy. Stevie tugged at Dan's sweater, and they broke apart long enough to pull the sweater over Dan's head. Stevie ran his hands greedily over Dan's bare skin as they kissed again.

Dan lifted him right off the floor without breaking the kiss. Stevie wrapped arms and legs around Dan as he carried Stevie to the bed. They fell together in a heap on top of the covers.

Dan was already working on the buttons of Stevie's shirt. Stevie helped him, and after a few fumbling minutes the shirt got tossed onto the floor. Dan immediately went for the button and zipper of Stevie's jeans.

"Jesus, Dan," Stevie gasped when Dan got his jeans open and started pulling them off. "Oh. Oh."

Dan grinned at him. "No underwear?"

"Feels good like that." Stevie pulled the crumpled jeans off with his toes and kicked them aside.

Dan's hot gaze swept down Stevie's naked body. The look in those dark eyes sent Stevie's pulse racing. He could hear the rush of blood in his head. When Dan's eyes met his again, brimming with lust and love, his breath caught in his chest.

"You're the most beautiful thing I've ever seen," Dan whispered.

Stevie blinked back tears. He reached up, cradled Dan's face in his hands. "Want you so fucking bad."

Dan bent and kissed him, sliding one hand up the inside of his thigh, urging his legs apart. He pulled back and nuzzled Stevie's neck, planting soft little kisses down his throat, biting gently at his collarbone. Stevie moaned when Dan sucked one nipple into his mouth, tongue working.

"Oh, Dan, oh, God, God that feels so good." Stevie arched against Dan's mouth.

Dan rolled, and Stevie's legs opened. Dan's body was a hot weight between his thighs. His hips moved of their own accord, rubbing his erection against Dan's ribs. Dan growled, lifted his head, and stared into Stevie's eyes.

"Been wanting to taste you for so long," Dan said, low and husky. He petted Stevie's belly, fingers stroking tantalizingly downward.

Stevie licked his lips. He could barely think, let alone make any words come out. "I ... oh ... there's ... in there ... shit, Dan."

Dan scooted down further, until his warm breath caressed Stevie's groin. Stevie lifted his hips, begging. Dan smiled up at him.

"You clean, Stevie?"

Stevie nodded "Yeah. Got my last test back just ... just the other day."

Dan smiled, slow and lustful. "Then we don't need condoms. I got tested last month, and I haven't been with anyone in ages."

He wrapped one big hand around Stevie's cock and rubbed his thumb over the head. Stevie gasped, digging his fingers into Dan's shoulders. Dan gave him a smile that melted him from the inside out, then bent and took Stevie into his mouth.

"Oh! Oh, fuck!" Stevie cried when Dan's tongue probed at his slit. He clenched his fingers in Dan's hair, dug his heels into the mattress, and tried hard not to shove his dick down Dan's throat.

Evidently Dan had other ideas. He opened wide and took Stevie deep, pulled back and swirled his tongue around the head, and swallowed him down again. He grabbed Stevie's hips, lifted them so that Stevie's cock hit the back of his throat, and that did it. Stevie let go of his control and fucked Dan's mouth like he'd dreamed of doing for months.

He heard someone babbling, incoherent words of love and want, and realized with a shock that it was him. He looked down; saw Dan's smoldering eyes locked onto his face, those sensual lips stretched around his cock. The sight sent him spiraling over the edge. He let out a long, wailing cry as he came in Dan's mouth.

Dan crawled up over Stevie's limp body and kissed him. Stevie opened wide for him, clutching him close. He could taste his own semen on Dan's tongue. "Fuck, Dan," he panted, pulling back to lick a trickle of come off the corner of Dan's mouth. "That was amazing. Just ... fucking amazing."

"You taste so good," Dan pushed the hair away from Stevie's face, kissed his eyelids, his nose, and his swollen cheek. "I could do that forever."

Stevie smiled, hooked a leg around Dan's waist, and pulled him down into another burning kiss. Dan moaned into his mouth, hips pushing against Stevie's leg. He could feel Dan's cock straining under the worn denim, and suddenly the need to have that cock in his mouth was unbearable. He pushed on Dan's chest, rolled him over and straddled his hips.

"Wanna suck you, Dan." He leaned down and sucked lightly at Dan's lower lip while he undid the button and zipper of Dan's threadbare jeans. He tugged at the soft fabric. "Off. Now."

Dan's eyes stared into Stevie's, bright with need. In the few seconds it took for them to get Dan's jeans and shoes off, Stevie was already getting hard again. He slithered down between Dan's legs, nibbling his muscled belly as he went. Dan spread his thighs wide, pushed up on his elbows, and looked at Stevie with eyes hot like lava.

"Do it, Stevie," Dan breathed, his voice hoarse. "Suck my cock."

Stevie thought he might come again just from the way Dan said that. He bit his lip and rubbed his cheek against Dan's thigh, trying to get hold of himself. He kissed his way up the inside of one thigh, then ran his tongue over Dan's balls before kissing down the other thigh. Dan trembled against him, legs opening wider, one hand raking through Stevie's hair. Stevie wrapped his fingers around Dan's wide shaft and stroked lightly. Dan let out a sharp little cry that shot through Stevie like an arrow. He looked up and thought he'd never seen anything as purely beautiful as Dan's face right then, flushed and dazed with desire.

"I love you, Dan." He stretched his jaw wide and swallowed Dan to the root.

"Oh! God, Stevie!" Dan's head fell back, his fingers clenched in Stevie's hair.

Stevie moaned with his mouth full. The taste of pre-come made his head spin. He worked lips and tongue up and down the length of Dan's prick, rolling Dan's balls gently between his fingers, and flicked his tongue into the slit every time he pulled back. His free hand dropped down almost of its own accord to stroke his own dick, which was fully erect again. When Dan jerked, cried out, and shot deep in his throat, it took every ounce of control Stevie had not to come himself.

He reluctantly let Dan slip out of his mouth and sat up. The sight of Dan sprawled on his back, flushed and panting with splayed legs and half-closed eyes, nearly shattered Stevie's control. He held on by sheer willpower.

"Oh. My God, Stevie." Dan reached out, took Stevie's hand, and pulled. Stevie went gladly into Dan's arms, resting his head on Dan's broad chest and curling his body around Dan's larger one.

"Good?" Stevie wound an arm around Dan's waist.

"Hell, 'good' doesn't come close. Try 'mind-blowing' and maybe you'll have it." Dan lifted Stevie's chin with one finger and gave him a long, languid kiss.

Stevie closed his eyes, letting his mind relax and float. He felt like he could lose himself forever in Dan's kiss. He pressed as close as he could, one leg thrown over Dan's groin so that his erection dug into Dan's hip. Dan chuckled against his lips.

"Ready to go again, huh?" Dan's hand wandered down to cup Stevie's balls.

"Yeah. Your fault, for being so goddamn sexy." Stevie plucked at Dan's nipple. Dan let out a sharp little sound. His cock twitched and started to swell against Stevie's thigh, and Stevie smiled. "Fuck me, Dan. I want you inside me."

Dan's eyes glazed over. "Oh. Um. Give me a minute?"

Stevie grinned at him. "I'll help you." He took Dan's swelling dick in his hand and leaned up so that his lips brushed Dan's ear. "I've wanted to have your cock in my ass since the first time I saw you. You'll fuck me good and hard, won't you? Just shove this big dick right up my ass and pound me good. I bet you'll fill me right up, stretch my asshole nice and tight." He stroked Dan a little faster, his grip a little firmer. "I want this hard cock fucking my ass. Want your come inside me. Want to feel it running out my hole and down my thighs."

Dan glanced from Stevie's face to his own fully renewed erection and back again with wide eyes. "Shit, you're good." He flashed a lustful grin. "You talking dirty is sexy as hell."

"Thought you'd go for that." Stevie didn't tell him that some men had paid extra for it. He reached to open the drawer of the little table beside the head of the bed, took out the lube, and handed it to Dan. "Can't wait anymore, Dan. I need it."

"God, me, too." Dan opened the tube and squeezed some into his hand. He reached behind Stevie, sliding two slick fingers along his crack and pushing inside in one swift motion.

"Oh, oh, yeah, yes, fuck!" Stevie cried. He was still lying with his chest pressed to Dan's and his leg thrown over Dan's thighs. He moved up to straddle Dan's hips, lifting his ass into the air. Dan pushed a third finger in easily, and Stevie felt himself opening right up.

"Want in now," Dan panted. Those dark eyes burned, penetrating Stevie every bit as much as the big fingers moving inside him. "Ride me."

Stevie didn't need to be asked twice. He sat up on his knees, grasped Dan's erection, and pressed the tip against his lube-slicked hole. They stared at each other. For a brief second, Stevie wondered if his own eyes looked as amazed and full of wonder as Dan's did. Then he lowered himself just as Dan pushed his hips up. Dan's thick cock slid all the way in, and he forgot about everything else.

He rode Dan hard and fast, hands braced on Dan's chest. Dan bent his knees and dug both heels into the mattress, slamming into Stevie's body so hard Stevie could feel the shock waves in his skull. Dan's big hand stroked Stevie's prick, squeezing tight. Stevie squirmed, spread, changed the angle until Dan's cock hit the sweet spot dead on. He gasped, head falling back, his entire body electrified. Pressure rose swiftly inside him, hot and sweet. He could feel Dan's shaft pulsing in his ass, and knew Dan was close, too.

Dan's eyes were locked onto his when Stevie's orgasm exploded through him, shaking him from head to foot and tearing a hoarse scream from his throat. His semen splashed onto Dan's stomach just as Dan shot inside him. He couldn't remember the last time he'd looked into a lover's eyes as he came. It felt so good to see the love in those big chocolate-brown eyes, mingling with the heat of sex.

"Oh. Oh, wow. Man." Dan's voice was breathless. He pulled Stevie down to him, stroking the damp curls away from his face. They kissed, soft and sated. "Stevie, you're amazing. Just ... wow."

Stevie caressed Dan's flushed cheeks, trailed kisses over his jaw, loving the way the stubble felt on his swollen lips. "Feels so good to have you inside me, Dan. Stay with me?"

Dan laughed. "You just try and make me leave." He lifted Stevie up enough to slide his softening dick out of his body and cuddled Stevie closer.

Stevie rested his cheek on Dan's chest and twined their legs together. "Hey, Dan?"

"Yeah?"

"I'm so happy right now."

Dan's warm chuckle rumbled wonderfully against Stevie's ear. "Me, too."

"Love you, Dan."

"Love you, too."

Stevie wondered briefly if they should get up and wash off, maybe brush their teeth. But Dan's arms were so warm and secure around him, and his heartbeat steady and comforting under Stevie's cheek, that moving seemed like too monumental a task. Dan's breathing was already becoming slow and even, his body relaxing in Stevie's arms. Stevie smiled, closed his eyes, and let sleep take him.

CHAPTER ELEVEN

When Dan woke, he thought he was still dreaming. It seemed to be the only explanation for the warm, naked body in his arms. And what a dream it had been. He could still see Stevie's face flushed with orgasm. Could still feel Stevie's body rippling around his cock, hot as a furnace and so tight.

He felt himself floating up into wakefulness. He didn't want to wake up. Didn't want to ever let go of that dream. But the white light of day glowed red through his stubbornly closed eyelids, and he knew it had to end. He sighed, started to sit up, and realized something was lying on top of his arm.

No, he thought. Not something. Someone.

Stevie.

It hadn't been a dream at all.

Dan's eyes flew open. Sunshine poured through the window, bathing the small room in brightness. Stevie lay on his side, with his back pressed tight against Dan's chest and both hands curled under his chin. His pale skin shone in the morning light, cheeks rosy with sleep, golden curls like a disheveled halo. If it hadn't been for the splashes of dried semen, he could've passed for a cherub.

Dan skimmed gentle fingers over the bruise on Stevie's cheek and clenched his jaw. The urge to find Jesse and pound his face into hamburger burned in his guts. His fingers twitched, and he relaxed them with a huge effort. If Stevie could let it go, so could he.

His right hand had gone numb from Stevie's weight on his arm. He wriggled his arm around, trying to free himself without waking Stevie. Murmuring something as he stirred, Stevie rolled onto his stomach. Dan pulled his arm free with a sigh of relief.

He sat up and shook his hand to get the circulation going, watching Stevie's back rise and fall with his breathing. The sheet had slipped down to expose the graceful curve of his buttocks.

That gorgeous expanse of back and ass was just too tempting. Dan leaned down and pressed a soft kiss between Stevie's shoulder blades.

That kiss turned into a whole series of kisses, trailing down the length of Stevie's spine. Stevie's skin was heated silk under Dan's lips and hands as he made his way downward, detouring now and then to kiss the faint brown scars left from the fat man's whip.

By the time he reached the swell of Stevie's ass, Dan was hard as steel, and he'd begun to suspect that Stevie was awake. That ragged sort of breathing usually didn't happen during sleep. He ran a finger lightly between Stevie's ass cheeks and grinned at the barely audible moan that elicited.

"Spread your legs," he said, very softly just in case Stevie really was asleep. "Stay on your stomach."

Stevie opened his thighs wide without rolling over. Dan chuckled. He moved to kneel between Stevie's legs. Seeing him like that, lying face down with eyes shut and legs open, nearly undid Dan. He ran his palms up Stevie's thighs, up over his smooth butt, across the small of his back and down the sides of his hips. He waited until Stevie's whole body trembled under his hands before he spread Stevie's ass cheeks apart.

"Oh, oh, oh, oh, please," Stevie moaned. He dug his fingers hard into the mattress, hips lifting off the bed. "Please, Dan."

The sight of that sweet little hole made Dan's mouth water. He bent and swirled his tongue around the petal soft skin, tasting sweat and come and Stevie. Stevie's body opened easily, hot and pulsing around his probing tongue. He lifted Stevie's hips and pushed three fingers in to the hilt. He wished he could bathe in the sounds Stevie made, sharp little sounds of pure need that fired Dan's brain and made his cock burn. He bit one firm cheek, just hard enough to make Stevie squeal.

"God, Dan," Stevie panted. "Fuck me, now, right now, please!"

Dan sat up on his knees and rubbed his prick against Stevie's balls. A tremor ran through Stevie's body. He scrambled onto hands and knees and stared over his shoulder at Dan, blue eyes bright and hot.

"Lube?" Dan said, frantically digging in the covers to find it.

"Here." Stevie lunged and grabbed the lube off the floor where it had fallen. Dan snatched it from him, got a palmful, slicked himself up, and impaled Stevie in one stroke.

"Oh, fuck," Dan growled. "God, you feel so good inside. God." He sank his fingers into Stevie's hips and bit his lip, not moving yet, just letting Stevie's heat seep through his skin.

Stevie whimpered and rocked back against him, forcing him in deeper. He watched his cock being enveloped by that pale, perfect ass. Stevie's hole stretched tight, tugging at him, and his control snapped. He got a good grip on Stevie's hip bones and fucked him hard and deep.

"Ooooo, oh, fuck yeah!" Stevie pushed up, reaching one arm behind him to wind around Dan's neck. Dan reached down and pumped Stevie's cock hard with one hand, buried the other in his tangled hair, and met Stevie's mouth with his.

Dan felt Stevie's dick swell in his palm. Stevie's body went rigid, his ass squeezed Dan's cock tight, and warm wetness flowed over Dan's hand. Dan came a split second later, groaning into Stevie's open mouth. He pulled out, and they collapsed into a sweaty, sticky heap.

"Oh, man," Stevie sighed after a few panting minutes. "That's the way to wake up." He wrapped himself around Dan's body, cuddling close. "I fucking love morning sex."

"Me, too." Dan traced a finger down Stevie's back, sliding it into his cleft to feel the come seeping out of Stevie's ass. "Didn't know that until just now, but yeah. I think I could get used to it."

Stevie pushed up on one elbow and gave Dan a surprised look. "You mean you never had morning sex until now?"

Dan flushed. "Never spent the night with anybody before."

"Oh, wow." Stevie laid a hand on Dan's cheek. The look in his eyes made Dan feel warm all over. Made him feel cherished. Something else he could get used to. "I'm sorry, Dan."

"What for? I'm not." Dan slipped his finger inside Stevie, just to watch Stevie's eyes darken. "You're the first guy I've ever wanted to spend the night with."

"Oh. Oh, um ... Oh." Stevie bit his lip when Dan pushed another finger in. "Shit, Dan, you're turning me on again."

Dan laughed. "Oh, now isn't that a shame? Wonder what we ought to do about that?"

Stevie gave him a grin that was pure evil. "Awful pretty mouth you got there, mister."

"Oh, yeah?"

"Yeah."

"So?"

"So." Stevie leaned down and bit Dan's nipple hard. Dan yelped.

"So what?" Dan twisted his fingers to hit the sweet spot and made Stevie moan.

"So, you should suck my cock." Stevie raised blazing blue eyes to Dan's face.

Dan grinned. "Bring it on up here."

* * * * *

Stevie had to rush to get ready for work. It was probably the shower that did it. When they'd finally hauled themselves out of bed and headed off to get clean, Stevie had forty-five minutes to get ready and get to work. By the time they stumbled out of the shower, the hot water had run cold and they were down to ten minutes. Dan put on his clothes from the night before and went to straighten the bed. That chore done, he sat down and watched with a smile as Stevie pulled on a pair of purple jeans while holding a half-eaten doughnut between his teeth.

"Not much of a breakfast, is it?" Dan said as Stevie stuffed the rest of the pastry in his mouth.

Stevie chewed and swallowed while buttoning his shirt. "I would've made a real breakfast, but we're kinda out of time now. Or, well, I am. You could go out or something." He snatched a red sneaker off the floor and pulled it on, hopping on one foot.

"Naw. I'll wait until sometime when you can go with me." Dan pulled Stevie down onto his lap. "Want me to drive you to the bookstore?"

"Oh, man, that'd be great!" Stevie tugged his other shoe on, twisted around and lifted his face for a kiss, which Dan happily gave him. "I've been walking on Saturdays, since John and Evan go over early, and I can't ride with them unless I want to go early, too, which I don't. I don't mind usually, but I have a feeling walking might not be so easy today."

"Oh, yeah? How come?"

Stevie stood up and gave Dan a stern look over his shoulder. "Oh, I wonder. Maybe the workout my ass has gotten in the last ... let's see ..." He made a show of checking his watch. "Not even twelve hours? Could that be it?"

Dan stood up, too, folded Stevie in his arms, and kissed his forehead. "I'm not sorry."

"Me neither. Even though I'm probably gonna walk bowlegged for a month." Stevie wound both arms around Dan's neck, pressing close. "I can't believe it's been less than a day."

"Know what you mean." Dan lifted Stevie's chin with his finger, and they kissed, a long, lazy kiss full of promise. "Don't wanna ever let you go."

Dan felt Stevie smile against his mouth. "Love you."

"Love you." Dan reluctantly pulled away. "We better go. Wouldn't want you to be late."

Stevie smiled, his face glowing with happiness. "I won't be late by much. 'Sides, they'll understand." He laced his fingers through Dan's and tugged him toward the door. "C'mon, let's go."

Dan smiled and followed Stevie out into the crisp October morning. He didn't mention the way his guts twisted at the thought of his relationship with Stevie being public knowledge. *Stop it*, he told himself sternly. *You owe it to him to be open about this thing. And if there's anyone that'll be cool about it, it's John and Evan. Start there, the rest'll come.*

"Dan? What're you thinking about?"

Dan met Stevie's brilliant blue gaze and smiled. "Just how happy I am."

Stevie's smile warmed Dan right down to his toes. "Me, too, Dan."

* * * * *

Stevie ended up being fifteen minutes late, and that was mostly because he insisted on Dan coming in with him and saying hi to John and Evan. The store's small parking lot was full, and Dan had to park a couple of blocks down the street.

Dan was nervous about being out in public for the first time as half of a gay couple, but he kept his fears to himself. He just couldn't bring himself to look into Stevie's big blue eyes, radiant with love and happiness, and refuse him anything. So they walked into Rainbow Books hand in hand, and Dan pretended his mouth wasn't bone dry from anxiety.

"Stevie! You're late, doll." John looked up from opening rolls of quarters into the cash drawer. His eyebrows disappeared under the hair hanging in his face when he saw Dan and Stevie holding hands and the angry red bruise on Stevie's cheek. "Well, never mind, I think I know what kept you. But what the hell happened to your face?"

Stevie wrinkled his nose. "Jesse happened. He didn't like me breaking up with him."

John frowned. "I knew that boy was trouble. You think he'll leave you alone?"

"He better, if he knows what's good for him." Dan said. "I'll break him in half if he ever lays a finger on Stevie again."

John laid a hand over his heart. "Oh, my. Stevie, honey, you better hold on to this one."

Stevie squeezed Dan's hand and gave him a smile that turned his knees to jelly. "I plan to."

"You could've taken the day off, sweetie. Stayed in bed." John gave them a wicked grin, and Dan blushed.

Stevie laughed. "No, I couldn't. Megan's off today, remember? No way could you handle the register and the customers by yourself."

"Hey, who do you think did it before you came along? Little elves?"

"It's way busier now, and you know it."

"Evan could've helped me."

John and Stevie both burst into giggles. Dan looked from one to the other, puzzled. John noticed his expression and leaned over the counter.

"Evan's hopeless out on the floor," John muttered. "Sometimes I think he fakes being so bad at it, because he is not fond of working with the public. He'd rather hide in that office and count our money."

"You know he does more than that," Stevie said, still giggling a little.

"I know. But if I didn't pick on him, he'd think I didn't love him anymore." John arched an eyebrow at Dan. "Speaking of which, Dan, I see you finally came to your senses."

Dan blushed even harder. "Yeah, I guess I did."

"Well, good for you both. You're so hot together, you should be in pornos."

"John!" Stevie laughed, glancing up at Dan's flaming cheeks. "I think you've embarrassed Dan enough for one day, huh?"

John tried, not very successfully, to look contrite. "Sorry, Dan sweetie."

Dan grinned. "Don't worry about it." He turned to Stevie. "I better go and let you get to work."

"Okay."

Dan hesitated just long enough to make sure no one but John was watching, then pulled Stevie close, tilted his face up, and kissed him quite thoroughly. It took a huge amount of willpower to make himself stop. He caressed Stevie's cheek, rubbing his thumb over that plump lower lip.

"I'll pick you up after work, what time do you get off?"

"Six." Stevie rose on tiptoe and kissed Dan again, a light brush of lips. "Love you."

"Love you, too. 'Bye." He let Stevie's hand slip out of his and backed away. "'Bye, John. Tell Evan I said hi, okay?"

"Sure thing, sugar," John said. "See you later."

Dan left the store with Stevie's kiss still tingling on his lips. He whistled to himself as he walked back to the Jeep, feeling light and a little dazed. He'd just kissed another man in public for the first time, and nothing had happened at all. Even though he hadn't seen anyone looking, the store was packed with people browsing among the shelves, so he figured someone must've seen. But nobody had cared in the least.

He felt more free at that moment than he ever had.

"Dan," he said to himself as he climbed behind the wheel of his Jeep and started it up, "I believe you can do this."

* * * * *

Dan headed home, changed clothes, and nuked two frozen sausage biscuits for a late breakfast. He sprawled on the sofa and flipped through the TV channels while he ate. But every show seemed hopelessly dull compared to the memories of making love with Stevie. Eventually he turned the TV off again.

He looked at the clock. Barely eleven. Seven more hours before Stevie would be off work. Seven more hours until he could hold Stevie again, kiss him, caress his soft, bare skin. It seemed like forever.

Just before noon, Dan had had enough. He shrugged his jacket on and headed out the door.

No one answered his knock at Carlos and Shawna's apartment. He got Melina's answering machine when he called her place, then the voice mail when he tried her cell phone.

"Damn." He clicked his own cell phone closed. "Oh, well. Guess you'll have to entertain yourself, Danny-boy."

After a few minutes of deliberation, he decided to head downtown. It was shaping up to be a gorgeous day, cool and sunny. A perfect day for roaming the colorful streets in the heart of the city, poking into all the little shops. He headed for his Jeep.

Wandering around Asheville kept him pleasantly occupied for several hours. He kept seeing things he wanted to share with Stevie: a neon-pink coat that was just his style, a barefoot girl with dreadlocks playing "Without You I'm Nothing" on an acoustic guitar, the way the bright leaves floated on the breeze and splashed the sidewalks with color. He strolled the busy streets with a smile, imagining the things Stevie would say and do if he were here.

A little after five, close to the time Stevie got off work, Dan decided to start back toward his Jeep. He carried a big bag full of varied treats from the candy barrels at Mast General Store, as well as two used CDs and a hot-pink, long-sleeved t-shirt with *Princess* spelled out across the front in rhinestones. Stevie would love it. He decided not to mention that he'd told the salesgirl it was for his girlfriend.

He was only a block from where he'd parked when he saw Jesse. The young man was standing in an alley off the main road, talking in low, urgent tones to a boy barely out of his teens with a hard face and cruel eyes. Dan clenched his fists. The urge to grab Jesse and throttle him was almost unbearable. The only thing keeping him from doing it was Stevie. If Stevie wanted it over and forgotten, then Dan would do it, no matter how much he itched for the satisfaction of punching Jesse's self-righteous face. He set his eyes firmly ahead and made himself walk past the alley. If Jesse saw him, he didn't let on.

By the time Dan got back to Rainbow Books, he'd managed to push Jesse to the back of his mind. He'd debated mentioning seeing him to Stevie, then decided not to. He didn't want Jesse tarnishing even a second of their time together. He found a space in the parking lot this time, locked the Jeep, and hurried inside, bringing the candy with him.

Stevie was nowhere to be seen when he walked in. Neither was John. Evan stood at the checkout counter, looking uncomfortable. Dan walked over with a smile.

"Hey, Evan," he said. "How're you doing?"

"I'm good, Dan." Evan reached across the counter to shake Dan's hand. "How are you?"

"I'm great, thanks. Just great. Where's John? And Stevie?"

"In the back. We just got a delivery. My back's been acting up lately, so they have to deal with the heavy lifting." Evan gave him a knowing smile. "So, I hear congratulations are in order for you and Stevie."

Dan blushed furiously, but couldn't stop the big grin from spreading over his face. "Yeah, I guess so. Thanks. I'm awfully happy about it."

"I can tell. Stevie's been floating on a cloud all day. Sorry about John this morning, by the way. Stevie told me what he said." Evan shook his head. "The man has no shame."

"It's okay. Wouldn't be John if he didn't say stuff like that, I guess."

"That's true. He's outspoken and flamboyant and very much an extrovert. Not like me at all." Evan leaned on his elbows and gave Dan a sharp look. "Correct me if I'm wrong, Dan, but it seems to me that you and Stevie fall into that category as well."

"What do you mean?"

"Well, you strike me as being a pretty private sort of person. I'm guessing you'd much rather be in the background than the focus of attention, am I right?"

"Yeah, that's pretty much on the money."

"As I thought. Stevie, however, is a lot like John. He's outgoing, sometimes he's outrageous, and he dresses to make people look at him. Plus, he's openly affectionate and doesn't care who's looking or what they think of it. Right?"

"Right again." Dan bit his lip and decided to take the plunge. "So how do you handle that? I mean, I love Stevie, more than anything, but I'm not sure I'm ready to be as open about it as he wants me to be. I just came out after spending my whole life lying about who I am. It's hard to change all that overnight, you know?"

Evan nodded. His dark eyes were sympathetic. "I know. The only real advice I can give you is to be honest with Stevie. Tell him how you feel. It truly won't occur to him to think you might want to keep a low profile, because that's just not in his nature, but I don't think he'll take it personally. He's a very generous and understanding young man."

"I know. I just don't want to hurt him."

"Understandable. But it'll hurt a lot more if this doesn't come out until it turns into a fight. This same type of situation nearly broke up John and me years ago when we first got together."

"What happened?"

"I didn't tell him that it made me uncomfortable for him to grope me in public, because I didn't want to hurt his feelings. It all came to a head at my sister's wedding reception. John was all over me, and people kept giving us those scandalized looks, and I just suddenly couldn't ignore it anymore. I blew up at him, yelled at him to stop touching me. He stopped, all right. For nearly a month. He left me and went to live in some fleabag hotel. Longest month of my life, trying to get used to waking up in the morning without him beside me."

Evan's eyes were soft and sad with the memory. Dan reached out without thinking and touched Evan's hand. "So how'd you get back together?"

"I eventually swallowed my pride, went to him, and told him I'd been an inexcusable prick and begged him to take me back. He said it was about time I apologized to him, because he'd been just about to break down and come to me. That was a lesson to us both. Since then, we've always told each other the truth. Because no matter how hurtful some things might seem at the time, nothing hurts as much as living without each other."

Dan nodded. "Thanks, Evan. You're all right."

Evan grinned. "So are you."

"Dan!"

Dan turned just in time to get a double armful of wildly excited Stevie. Dan wrapped his arms around Stevie and nuzzled his hair. "Hey, Stevie."

"Hey, sexy." Stevie pulled Dan's face to his and kissed him deeply. "God, I missed you."

"Missed you, too." Dan kissed Stevie's nose, then gently pried him loose.

Stevie twined his fingers around Dan's. "So what'd you do today?"

"Nothing much. Couldn't stand being by myself in the apartment, and nobody was home, so I went downtown and hung out for a while." Dan held up the bag of candy. "Got some goodies at Mast General."

"Cool!" Stevie snatched the bag out of his hand and started digging through it. "Oh, man, giant peppermint sticks! I love these things!" He pulled a large red and white-striped candy stick out of the bag, unwrapped it, and stuck one end in his mouth.

John appeared from around a shelf at that moment and smiled when he saw Dan. "Hi, sweetie! Got any candy for Uncle John?"

Stevie pulled the peppermint stick out of his mouth. "Hands off, it's mine!"

Dan laughed. "I think there's enough for everybody." He held the bag out to John.

"Thanks, honey." John took a candied grapefruit slice, arching an eyebrow at Stevie while he unwrapped it. "No more candy for you, little boy. It makes you mean."

"Better believe it." Stevie sucked on the end of the peppermint, giving John a fierce look.

Dan watched the candy stick sliding in and out of Stevie's soft mouth, and suddenly wanted very much to be alone with him.

"So," he said, hoping he didn't sound as aroused as he felt, "you off yet?"

"I got a few more minutes." Stevie swirled his tongue around the candy, blue eyes blandly innocent.

"For God's sake, go on," John said. "If I have to watch any more of this foreplay I'll be forced to assault Evan right here at the counter, and he'll never forgive me."

Stevie widened his eyes. "I don't know what you're talking about, John. I'm just enjoying a nice piece of candy." He licked the entire length of the peppermint stick, then deep-throated it.

Dan turned twenty shades of red, but his need to get Stevie naked far outstripped his embarrassment. He grabbed Stevie's free hand and started pulling him toward the door. "Well, if it's okay with y'all, I think we'll be heading out. 'Bye, guys."

"Take tomorrow afternoon off, Stevie," Evan called. "Megan's here, we'll be fine."

"Cool, thanks!" Stevie waved at them over his shoulder. "'Bye!"

Dan caught Evan's eye and smiled at him, then pulled Stevie out the door.

They got all the way to the Jeep before Dan lost the battle with his rising desire. He pushed Stevie up against the Jeep's door, pulled the candy out of his mouth, and kissed him hard and deep.

"Need to fuck you," Dan growled.

"Shit, yeah." Stevie hooked an ankle around Dan's leg and humped against him. "Your place or mine?"

"Yours is closer."

"Closer's good."

"Get in the car."

"It's not a car, it's a Jeep."

Dan laughed. "Get in the Jeep, then. Smart ass."

Stevie grinned, opened the door, and slid over to the passenger seat. Dan climbed in beside him and spent the next couple of minutes trying desperately to watch the road instead of Stevie, who was rubbing himself through his jeans while enthusiastically sucking his peppermint stick. Dan sighed with relief when he pulled the Jeep into the little parking space beside John and Evan's garage and killed the engine.

"Damn, Stevie. You sure don't make it easy to drive."

Stevie slithered onto his lap, straddling his hips. "That was bad, huh?"

"Very."

"Whatcha gonna do about it?"

Dan raised his eyebrows, surprised by what Stevie seemed to be implying. "Well, I don't know." Dan spoke slowly, testing the waters. "Guess maybe I need to teach you a lesson."

Stevie's eyes glinted with a dark hunger, and Dan knew he'd been right about what Stevie wanted. The knowledge went straight to his dick, bringing him painfully erect between one heartbeat and the next.

"You're right," Stevie said. "I need to be taught a lesson." He leaned forward and nipped at Dan's upper lip. "So take me inside and teach me."

It was all Dan could do to control himself until they got inside. He followed Stevie up the stairs to the apartment, watching that sweet little ass move and aching to touch it. The second the door was safely locked behind them, Dan tossed the bag of candy onto the table, then picked Stevie up and carried him to the armchair by the window. He set Stevie on his feet again, dug the lube out of the nightstand, and sat down in the chair.

"Pull your pants down," he ordered, "And keep that candy in your mouth."

Stevie undid his jeans and shoved them down his thighs, still sucking on his candy. His eyes gleamed. Dan licked his lips at the sight of Stevie's erection jutting between his shirt and open jeans. He wanted badly to touch, but he resisted.

"That's nice," Dan said, a little hoarsely. "On my lap now. Face down."

Stevie shuffled over and draped himself across Dan's lap. He gave Dan a long, smoldering stare over his shoulder. "Spank me good."

Dan stared into Stevie's eyes and suddenly couldn't believe he was doing this. He'd never spanked anyone, never wanted to. Never thought himself capable of wanting such a thing. It scared him more than a little.

"Dan?" Stevie's voice was gentle. "You don't have to."

Dan swallowed. "Sorry, Stevie. I just can't."

Stevie gave him a sideways smile. "It's okay. I like it now and then, when it's somebody I know I can trust, but it's no big deal."

He started to sit up. Dan put a hand firmly between his shoulder blades, keeping him down. "Didn't say you could get up."

Stevie's cheeks went pink. "Oh. Okay."

Dan's heartbeat tripped, stumbled, and picked up its rhythm in double time. Dominance and submission games were new territory for him, and Stevie's willingness to submit excited him beyond belief. The raw lust in Stevie's eyes gave him the confidence to follow his desires. He caressed Stevie's bare butt with his open palm.

"This pretty little ass is mine." Dan was vaguely surprised to hear himself saying such a thing. "Isn't it?"

"Fuck, yeah," Stevie said. "All yours."

"Mmmm." Dan spread Stevie's buttocks, bent down, and flicked his tongue over the rosy little opening. Stevie let out a sharp cry, hips lifting up to meet Dan's tongue. "This hole's just for me. My cock's the only one that gets to use it, isn't that right?"

"Oh. Yeah. Yours, Dan. Yours."

"Mine."

Dan flipped open the cap on the lube and squirted some onto his fingers. Letting the tube drop to the floor, he gently rubbed lube on Stevie's opening, circling his fingertips in a feather-light touch that had Stevie squirming helplessly on his lap.

"Oh. Please. Dan, please," Stevie begged. "Please."

"Please, what?" Dan pushed lightly against Stevie's hole. "Tell me."

Stevie licked his lips. "Stick your fingers in me. God, please."

Dan slipped a finger inside, found Stevie's prostate and nudged it. Stevie cried out.

"You like that, huh?" Dan added a second finger and began to slowly move, twisting and sliding. "You like me to finger your ass like that?"

"Yeah. Yeah, fuck. Oh."

Stevie's voice was rough, his face flushed. One end of the peppermint stick was clutched in his hand, while he sucked absently at the other end. Dan watched Stevie's lips and tongue caress the candy, and suddenly a wicked thought struck him. He pulled his fingers out of Stevie's ass.

"On the floor," he ordered before Stevie could react. "Bend over."

Stevie hurried to obey. He fell in a heap on the floor at Dan's feet, got his knees under him, and stuck his butt up in the air. Dan groaned out loud. There was something wonderfully decadent about Stevie on all fours on the floor, with his pants around his thighs and his shirt riding up his back, his hole stretched just slightly from Dan's fingers.

"Christ," Dan breathed. "Goddamn, that's hot. Um. Gimme that candy."

Stevie pulled the candy stick out of his mouth with an audible pop, then handed it behind him to Dan. The look in his eyes said he knew what Dan was about to do.

Dan grinned. He stuck the candy in his own mouth, sliding his tongue around it, making sure there were no sharp edges. It was absolutely smooth, slicked and tapered by Stevie's mouth. Perfect. Dan sucked until it was slippery with sugar syrup, then pulled it out of his mouth and inserted it into Stevie's ass.

"Oh, oh, God!" Stevie gasped. He rocked back, forcing the candy stick deeper inside him.

"You like that?" Dan asked, his voice tight with excitement. "You like having that up your butt?"

"Yeah. God."

"Well, don't get too used to it." Dan got a good grip on the peppermint stick and pumped it in and out, slowly. "It's only opening you for my dick."

Stevie moaned. "Even better."

That was it. Dan couldn't stand it anymore. "I gotta fuck you right now. Take that peppermint stick out of your ass."

Stevie reached back, jerked the candy out, and sent it skidding across the floor. "Fuck me, now, now, now!" He wiggled his butt invitingly.

"Aren't you supposed to be the one doing what I say?" Dan slipped a hand between Stevie's legs and gave his balls a gentle tug.

"Oh! God, do that again."

Dan did it again. "'Cause it sure sounds an awful lot like you're giving me orders."

Stevie let out an impatient growl. "Less talking, more fucking."

Dan grinned. "Whatever you say." He bent and stuck his tongue in Stevie's temptingly open hole. It tasted like peppermint, which seemed so odd that he started laughing.

"Dan!" Stevie whined. "Come on, c'mon, c'mon!" He twisted around and gave Dan a frantic look.

Dan opened his jeans and shoved them down. He coated himself with lube, positioned his cock at Stevie's entrance, and slid solidly home.

"Oh, oh, Stevie." He leaned over Stevie's back, supporting himself on his hands, and nuzzled Stevie's silky curls. "God."

Stevie arched back to rub his cheek against Dan's. "Fuck me now."

Dan kissed Stevie's neck and happily obliged him.

* * * * *

By the time they took a break, it was well into the night and dinnertime was long gone. They lay in each other's arms on the braided rug, exhausted and sated.

"Hey, Dan?" Stevie mumbled against Dan's chest.

"Hm?"

"'M hungry."

"Me, too."

Neither moved. Dan floated in a comfortable half-awake, half-asleep state, feeling lazy and content. A loud rumbling shook him out of his doze. He cracked an eye open and smiled down at Stevie.

"Was that you?"

Stevie propped his chin on his hand and gave Dan a sheepish grin. "Yeah. I'm really starved."

"I could about eat a horse myself."

"I'm too tired to cook. You wore me out."

"Don't cook. We'll order in." Dan pushed Stevie gently off and stood up. "What do you feel like having?"

Stevie lay back on the rug, brow furrowed in thought. "What about that new Chinese place? It's only a few minutes away, and their menu says they deliver."

"Suits me." Dan nudged Stevie with his toe. "Where's the menu?"

"Side of the fridge."

Dan shuffled into the kitchenette and pulled the menu out from under the Gay Pride magnet holding it in place. "So what's good?"

"Don't know, I haven't eaten there yet." Stevie pushed himself to his feet, came to Dan and wound both arms around him. "Kiss me."

Dan did. Stevie tasted like sex and peppermint. "Mm. How the hell'd I ever live before you came along, Stevie?"

Stevie laughed. "Sweet-talker. I love you."

"Love you, too, babe."

Dan kissed Stevie's smiling mouth one more time. Stevie snuggled close, cheek pressed to Dan's chest. Dan closed his eyes and rested his face against Stevie's hair. This, he thought, is worth any amount of public embarrassment.

He hoped he could remember that when the pressure was on.

CHAPTER TWELVE

Stevie loved Sunday mornings. Especially in the fall, when the bite in the air and the wind-tossed leaves outside made the bed seem even cozier. And now, the best reason of all to love Sunday mornings was lying next to him, pressed against his back, one golden-brown arm slung possessively around him. Stevie sighed in utter content and smiled at the bright morning outside his window.

He'd almost drifted back to sleep again when he realized Dan was awake. He could feel the change in the way Dan's body came alive against his. Dan's hips pressed against his ass, and his hand slipped between Stevie's legs. Suddenly Stevie was as hard as Dan. Dan's fingers slicked with saliva opened him easily. He arched his back, and Dan's cock slid inside him.

They moved together, taking their time, wrapped in a warm cocoon of pleasure. No time, no world, nothing but the two of them, caught up in the sweet, languid rhythm of Sunday morning lovemaking. Dan turned Stevie's face to his, and they kissed through the orgasms that shook them within seconds of each other.

"Good morning, Dan," Stevie said when he could talk again. He turned in Dan's arms and snuggled against his broad chest.

"Morning." Dan folded Stevie tightly against him and kissed his forehead. "I sure do like waking up this way."

"Me, too. So you wanna stay in bed all day, or go do something?"

"Hm. Well, keeping you right here is awfully tempting."

"It's sure as hell tempting me."

"But, I've got an idea."

"Oh, yeah? What?"

Dan gave him a wide grin. "Let's go hiking."

Stevie raised his eyebrows. "Hiking?"

"Yeah. I know a place."

"What sort of place?"

"A place not many people know about." Dan rolled Stevie on top of him and ran both hands down his back. "A nice, quiet, private place."

"Sounds interesting." Stevie bent and kissed Dan's chin. "We can have a picnic. I've even got a bottle of wine we can bring."

"Can I lick it off you?"

"Fuck yeah, you can."

Dan laughed, tangled a hand in Stevie's hair, and pulled him into another kiss. Stevie closed his eyes and melted, letting the sheer bliss of being in Dan's arms float him away.

* * * * *

It was almost noon by the time they finally left the apartment and climbed into Dan's Jeep. The backpack Stevie had loaded with sandwiches, chips, apples, and a bottle of local Riesling sat between his feet on the floorboard as they drove through town and out into the countryside. Stevie's spirits rose higher with every mile of winding road they traveled.

After nearly an hour of climbing higher into the mountains, Dan eased the Jeep onto a rutted dirt lane that twisted deep into the red-orange autumn forest. Stevie gazed curiously around him as Dan parked the Jeep on a flat spot by the side of the road.

"Wow, cool." Stevie climbed out and hefted the backpack. The day was unseasonably warm, perfect for hiking.

"Trailhead's just up the road, around that curve there." Dan pointed a few yards ahead. "Here, give me that backpack."

"I can carry it," Stevie protested as Dan lifted it right off of his shoulder.

"It's gonna get heavy before we get there." Dan slipped his arms through the straps and grinned. "Besides, I want to watch you."

"Watch me what?" Stevie laughed as they started up the road.

"Watch you walk."

"Oh, I get it. You want to stare at my ass the whole time."

"Yup."

"I can understand that. I mean, it's not like you've seen much of it lately."

"I plan on seeing lots more of that fine ass." Dan leaned down and licked Stevie's ear. "When we get to where we're going, first thing I'm gonna do is get you naked and fuck you raw."

Stevie's knees almost went at that. He looked up into Dan's eyes, and the heat there made him burn all over. He pulled Dan's face down and kissed him hard. "In that case, mister, you better start walking really, really fast, 'cause I need it pretty damn soon."

"You may as well settle down. We got about a half hour's hike ahead, and some of it's a little rough."

"Oh, man. You trying to wear me out?"

"Not by walking. Don't worry, you can handle it, it's not that hard."

Stevie gave Dan an evil grin. "Yeah, it is."

"Boy, you have a one-track mind." Dan popped him on the butt. "And am I ever glad you do. Now, shake a leg. You've got me needing it, too."

It actually took them closer to forty-five minutes to get to the end of the trail, mostly because Stevie kept veering off to investigate the shadowed hollows between boulders, or a sunlit clearing, or a tiny waterfall trickling over mossy rocks. He rapidly forgot all about sex in the thrill of discovery. This was the first time he'd been outside the city since he came to Asheville, and the forest enchanted him at every turn. Red, yellow, and orange leaves covered the forest floor, and the air smelled like rich earth and fast-flowing rivers. The half-bare trees sighed in the breeze overhead, dappling the world in an ever changing pattern of light and shade. Stevie felt like a little boy again, exploring the wilds and inventing adventures in his head.

Dan followed him, long legs pacing slow and steady while Stevie scampered around like a squirrel, exclaiming over this and that as he went. When they reached a bend in the trail, rounding a boulder that towered over their heads and overhung the path, Dan stopped Stevie from bounding ahead with a hand on his shoulder.

"Wait," Dan said. "Let's go together. I want to see your face."

Stevie's eyes widened. "Oh, are we there? Is this it?"

Dan nodded, and held out his hand. "C'mon."

Stevie intertwined his fingers with Dan's. Dan smiled at him, dark eyes sparkling with excitement. Stevie followed him around the bend, under the rock overhang, and out into brilliant sunshine. His mouth fell open and he stared, speechless.

They were standing on a wide rock ledge, with the big boulder at their backs. To the left, the mountain rose straight up, scraggly grasses clinging to the bare rock. To the right, the trail continued for a few yards before disappearing into a wide stretch of knee-high yellow grass.

It was the view directly ahead, though, that stole Stevie's breath. The mountain dropped away no more than five feet from where they stood, sheer and dizzying. A carpet of red, orange, and gold blanketed the valley far below and climbed the rounded peaks on the other side.

Stevie thought he'd never in his life seen anything so beautiful. The Rockies where he'd grown up had their own sweeping, clean-lined beauty. But this was something else again, all lush curves and bursting with life. Stevie shook his head.

"Oh, my God, Dan," he said, his voice soft and reverent. "This is ... amazing." He leaned back against Dan's solid warmth.

Dan put both arms around Stevie's waist and kissed his neck. "Gorgeous, huh?"

"Incredible." Stevie twisted around, lifting his face to receive Dan's kiss.

Dan patted Stevie's ass, then pulled away, tugging on his hand. "Come on, let's go to the meadow."

Stevie eyed the sheer drop-off to his left with a mix of awe and trepidation as he followed Dan down the rock path. He kept Dan's hand clutched in his. "How'd you find this place?"

"My cousins and I used to come here when we were kids. My uncle Rollin's house wasn't far from here. Just a little ways down the road from where we turned off, matter of fact. My mom and dad came to visit a lot. My mom's family was always real close."

Stevie watched Dan's back thoughtfully. "It must've been great. Wandering around the woods, I mean. Finding places like this. It sounds like so much fun."

"It was." Dan squeezed his hand, turned and smiled at him. "We had some good times."

"Do you still get together with your cousins?"

"Naw. Uncle Rollin died when I was fifteen, and Aunt Sarah couldn't keep up with the taxes on the land after that. She sold it the year after he died, and they all moved to Charlotte." Dan turned and gave him a sad little smile as they entered the meadow. "I miss them sometimes."

"I bet." Stevie reached up to wind his arms around Dan's neck. "I wish I'd known you then. I wish I could've seen you running around up here when you were a kid."

Dan grinned. "I wanna see you running around up here now. Bare." He tugged on Stevie's shirt. "Strip."

Stevie laughed, stood on tiptoe, and brushed a light kiss across Dan's lips. "You know what? I never saw a place I'd rather be naked in than this."

Stevie headed into the swaying golden grasses, shedding his shirt as he went. He could hear Dan's slow, measured footsteps right behind him. He turned and held Dan's gaze as he pulled off his sneakers and shimmied out of his jeans.

Dan raked molten eyes down Stevie's naked body. "You sure look good like that."

Stevie took Dan's hand, turned, and waded deeper into the meadow, pulling Dan with him. He smiled over his shoulder. "Let's make love, Dan. Here in the grass."

"Stevie," Dan said as he set the backpack down and started taking off his clothes, "you read my mind."

The cool breeze sighing through the grass made Stevie's spirit sing. Bared to the elements, wind in his hair and sun warming his skin, he felt fierce and free and wild. And Dan ... Dan looked like a god. Hard, sleek muscles under caramel skin, his erection dark and proud, brown eyes full of fire. Stevie sank to his knees and rubbed his lips against the tip of Dan's cock. Dan groaned.

"Tastes so good," Stevie murmured. "Love your cock."

Dan buried his hands in Stevie's hair. "Suck me, Stevie."

Stevie gladly obeyed. He took Dan slowly in, tongue and throat working, feasting on the feel and taste and smell of Dan's arousal. *So damn good. Dan's pre-come*, he thought, *must be the nectar of the gods. Because Dan's a god. A wild god of the wild woods. And I'm the god's lover. A sort of priest. And a priest has to be baptized, right?*

He pulled back, running with the idea as soon as it popped into his head. Dan moaned in frustration.

"Don't stop," Dan begged, his voice tight and breathless.

"Baptize me." Stevie wrapped a hand around Dan's shaft and started pumping.

Dan's expression said he wanted to be confused, but was too far gone right then to care. His hand joined Stevie's, and seconds later, he threw his head back and shouted as he came. His semen splattered onto Stevie's upturned face and into his open mouth. Stevie licked it off his lips, laughing.

Dan dropped to the ground beside Stevie. "Damn," he gasped. "What the hell was that all about?" He gave Stevie a dazed grin, eyes twinkling.

"You're a god, Dan. And I'm your priest. So I needed to be baptized." Stevie wiped a blob of come off one eyelid and licked it off his fingers.

"What?" Dan laughed.

Stevie pushed Dan onto his back and straddled him. "It's being naked outside. It makes me think weird stuff."

"Yeah, I see that."

"Hey, if you don't want me think things like that, then you shouldn't look so god-like, huh?"

Dan chuckled and shook his head. "Crazy boy. Now get off me and lie down."

"Okay. How long before you can get it up again?" Stevie settled onto his back in the cool grass and peered up at Dan with a smile.

"Smart ass." Dan pushed Stevie's thighs apart. Stevie could feel those dark eyes on him. "Wanted to see you like this, all spread out naked in the grass." Dan raised his eyes to Stevie's face. The mix of heat and tenderness there made Stevie's chest tight. "You're so beautiful, Stevie. I think you belong out here."

"Dan, I love you." Stevie reached down and started stroking himself. "Now do something about this!"

Dan laughed out loud. "I'd sure like a taste of that, if you think that'll take care of you."

"Hell, yeah. Your humble priest gives the gift of his seed as an offering to his own private sex god." Stevie lifted his hips, loving the way Dan's eyes grew heavy at the sight. "Take it."

Dan did take it. He swallowed Stevie whole, using lips, tongue, and a hint of teeth, and three fingers buried to the hilt in Stevie's ass, massaging the sweet spot. Stevie stared up into the bright blue sky, dotted with cottony puffs of cloud and wheeling birds, and wondered if he'd fallen into another world. An alternate universe of sun and breeze and beauty, of naked bronze-skinned gods with warm wet mouths and magic fingers. His fists tightened in Dan's hair, back arching as he came in Dan's mouth.

Dan pulled Stevie into his arms, and they lay wound together in the cool grass, skin to skin, kissing and caressing. Stevie felt safe and sheltered and utterly content with Dan's body pressed against his, those strong arms holding him close.

"Mm," Dan sighed. "This is nice."

"Sure is." Stevie snuggled closer, throwing a leg over Dan's thighs. "Let's not ever leave."

Dan's laugh rumbled in Stevie's ear, making him smile. "It'll get cold up here after dark. And we only brought enough food for one meal. Speaking of which, you wanna eat now? I'm hungry."

"Yeah, okay. I'm kind of hungry, too." Stevie sat up, reached across Dan's body and heaved the backpack over. "Damn, that's heavy. Okay, I made turkey sandwiches, and I've got potato chips and some apples and the wine. No cups, sorry. We'll have to drink out of the bottle."

Dan sat up and rummaged through the bag until he found the corkscrew. "You got no refinement, boy."

"Aw, no way! I've got culture out the ass!"

"Yeah, see what I mean? Not a refined thing to say." Dan popped the cork free and pointed it accusingly at Stevie. "Rough as a cob, my mama would've said."

"Am not. Gimme that." Stevie snatched the bottle out of Dan's hand and took a long, deep swallow.

"I take it all back," Dan said, grinning. "Nothing more cultured than sitting naked in a meadow on a mountain top, drinking wine right out of the bottle."

"Hey, this is good wine. Cost me twelve dollars."

"Well, there you go."

Stevie handed the bottle back to Dan and started setting food out on the giant towel he'd brought for a picnic blanket. "Evan's thinking about setting up a coffee shop in the bookstore."

"Oh, yeah?" Dan took a huge bite of sandwich. "Since when?"

"For a long time, he said. He's been seriously looking into it since he found out I could cook."

"What's that got to do with it?"

"He figures I could make cookies and stuff, too." Stevie bit into an apple and chewed thoughtfully for a moment. "I could do that. Might be fun."

Dan nodded, taking a swallow of wine. "I bet you'd get twice the customers. And that's saying something, busy as it's been there lately."

"Yeah. That'd be great. I really love it there, especially when it's real busy. I love to talk to the customers." Stevie stuffed a handful of chips into his mouth and crunched noisily. "You know what, sometimes I think about how much my life's changed in the last few months, and I can't believe it."

Dan gazed thoughtfully at him. "Does it bother you to talk about those days, Stevie? 'Cause there's something I been wanting to ask you about ... well, you know. What you used to do."

Stevie's guts twisted. He picked up the wine bottle and took a long drink to cover his hesitation. *It's only natural,* he told himself, *that Dan would be curious about it.* He made himself meet Dan's eyes and smile.

"Well, it's not my favorite subject, but yeah, we can talk about it. What'd you want to know?"

Dan reached out and took Stevie's hand, winding their fingers together. "Okay. I hope this doesn't sound stupid. But, it seems to me that you like sex plenty. Good thing for me, since I can't get enough of you." Dan smiled sweetly at him, and he smiled back, squeezing Dan's fingers. "What I'm wondering is, how'd you spend all that time having sex with strangers for money, and still love sex as much as you do? Especially the kinky stuff, like spanking. If it was me, I don't think I'd want to do that anymore."

Stevie looked down at the ground. "It was all just business, you know? I guess I just distanced myself from it. Which wasn't easy when they wanted me to top, or when they wanted me to come, but you do what you have to." He met Dan's gaze again. The dark eyes were curious, but held no hint of reprimand. "Most guys just wanted a straight vanilla fuck. Some of them wanted me to pretend to be jailbait, but even then, they just wanted me to blow them or let them fuck me. I could count the ones that wanted kink on my hands and have fingers left over. Roy had other boys who liked that sort of thing, so they usually got those jobs. I usually got the ones that just wanted somebody pretty."

"Except that one, the night before I found you." Dan shook his head. "This is gonna sound weird, but much as I'd like to bust that asshole's face for him, I'm kind of glad he hired you that night. 'Cause if he hadn't, I never would've met you."

The look in Dan's eyes made Stevie melt inside. He crawled over and climbed onto Dan's lap. "It's not weird. I've thought the same thing sometimes. Horrible as that night was, I wouldn't be here right now if it hadn't happened."

Dan cradled Stevie's face in both hands and kissed him. "I love you, Stevie."

"I love you, too." Stevie pinched Dan's nipple and smiled at the resulting groan. "So. Finish eating first, or fuck like bunnies first?"

"Hm. Can't we do both at the same time?" Dan gnawed at Stevie's neck. "Still hungry."

Stevie giggled and tried to pry Dan's teeth away. "Wasn't that a Seinfeld episode?"

"Think so, yeah." Dan scooped Stevie up in his arms, laid him down in the grass, and plopped down on top of him.

"Didn't work out well, if I remember right." Stevie pushed on Dan's chest. "You're heavy!"

"Aw, poor baby." Dan pushed up on his elbows. "That better?"

"Yeah." Stevie squirmed his legs out from under Dan's weight and locked his ankles around Dan's back. "Food can wait. Fuck me."

Dan laughed. "Rough as a cob," he teased. But he reached for the lube anyway.

* * * * *

The sun was setting by the time they got back to Stevie's apartment. Stevie had decided to stay the night with Dan, but wanted to stop by his place and get clothes and other supplies first. He left Dan in the Jeep while he raced upstairs to pack a bag.

The phone started ringing before he got to his door. He took the remaining stairs two at a time, hurriedly unlocked the door, and lunged for the phone.

"'Lo?" he panted.

"Stevie? Did I call at a bad time? You sound out of breath."

Stevie laughed at the suggestion in John's voice. "I had to run for the phone. Me and Dan went hiking, we just got back."

"Oh! Well, don't I have good timing?"

"Yeah, especially since I'm headed out the door again soon as I pick up a couple of things. I'm staying over with Dan tonight."

John chuckled. "Well, you know I'll expect full details later, sugar."

"Of course. So, did you just call to say hi, or what?"

"'Fraid not, sweetheart. There was a man here a little while ago looking for you. He said he'd been to your place and you weren't there, so he came here to the store. I wanted to call and let you know."

Stevie frowned at the wall. "Who was it?"

"He didn't say. But I thought he must be a friend, since he knew where you lived."

"What'd he look like?"

"Um. Let's see. Middle-aged, short, and skinny. Dark hair with lots of gray. And sweetie, I don't mean to tell you how to pick your friends, but he didn't seem like the nicest person in the world to me. He smiled a lot, but his eyes were mean."

Stevie leaned against the wall, feeling sick and dizzy. John had just described the man who'd owned him for a whole year.

Roy had found him.

"Stevie? Honey, are you there?"

"Yeah. Yeah, I'm here." Stevie headed for the closet and started pulling clothes out. "Listen, John? If that guy comes looking for me again, tell him I left, will you? Tell him I moved to another city or something."

"I'd be happy to. I didn't like the look of him at all."

"I don't want him to find me, John. I ... I'm afraid of him. I'm afraid he'll try to hurt me."

John's voice grew hushed and concerned. "Baby, did he do something to you? I just knew he was a bad guy."

"He kind of did, yeah. I don't want to go into details, if that's okay. But I can't let him find me."

"Sweetie, he won't find out from me and Evan. You go on and stay with Dan. And honey, don't travel to or from work alone, okay? If Dan can't ferry you, call me, and I'll do it. Matter of fact, don't come in to work tomorrow. Stay at Dan's place. We'll come over there after we close the store and work out a plan."

"Okay. Thanks, John. You guys are the best."

"I know, sugar. Now go on and get packed and get out of there! I won't worry about you if you're with Dan, he'll protect you."

"I'm gone right now. 'Bye, John."

"'Bye, sweetie."

Stevie hung up the phone, slung his bag over his shoulder, and headed for the Jeep, locking the door securely behind him.

"What took so long?" Dan asked as Stevie jumped in.

"John called right when I was walking through the door." Stevie latched his seatbelt and relaxed against the seat. "Roy came looking for me, Dan."

"What?" Dan glanced over at Stevie with wide eyes. "That bastard knows where you work?"

"And where I live, yeah. He told John he came here first, and I wasn't home, so he went to Rainbow Books." Stevie rubbed both hands over his eyes. "Glad I wasn't there. Damn. How the fuck did he find me?"

Dan chewed his lip, brow furrowed. He remembered seeing Jesse in that downtown alley the day before, and he wondered.

"Stevie, did you ever tell Jesse about what you used to do?"

Stevie twisted around to stare at him. "No. Why?"

Dan glanced at him again. "When I was downtown yesterday, I saw Jesse. He was in an alley with some rough-looking kid. Looked to me like he was telling the kid something important. Didn't think anything of it at the time, other than how much I wanted to kick his lousy ass. But just now I wondered if he might've been sending a message to Roy about you. I guess he couldn't have been, though, if he didn't even know about it."

"I bet that's exactly what he was doing, the fucker. I bet he found out somehow, and he sent Roy after me. Wouldn't surprise me any if they'd done business before. Jesse and me were never exclusive. Well, not on his part anyhow." Stevie sighed. "Shit. What am I gonna do, Dan?"

"For one thing, I think you should move back in with me."

"I think you're right."

"And no more riding the bus, ever. I'm driving you to work and picking you up after."

"That's what John said, too. And he told me to take tomorrow off. He and Evan are gonna come over after the store closes so we can work out a way to keep me from having to travel alone. Damn, I hate this." Stevie reached over and squeezed Dan's thigh. "But I'm glad I have you, Dan. You make me feel safe."

Dan took Stevie's hand in his. "I won't let anything happen to you, Stevie."

Stevie smiled. "I know."

Stevie clung to Dan's hand and tried not to think of the other things Jesse could've told Roy. *It's okay*, he told himself, *I'm safe with Dan. Roy won't find me.*

After a while, he almost believed it.

CHAPTER THIRTEEN

"Dan! Wake up, *amigo!*"

Dan shook off the memory of Stevie running naked through the sunlit meadow, laughing, bits of grass in his hair, and looked up at Carlos. "Sorry, what?"

Carlos laughed. "I asked you to hand me that level. That's the third time, too, man, where the hell's your mind today?"

"Got lots to think about. Sorry." Dan picked the level up off the work table and handed it to Carlos, who was perched at the top of a stepladder.

"No kidding." Carlos set the level on the shelf he'd just finished hanging, nodded, and looked down at Dan. "You've been on another planet all morning. What happened this weekend? You ever gonna tell me?"

Dan glanced around. The rest of the crew was scattered around the work site of the house they were remodeling, most of them working on the sun room and deck. He and Carlos were alone in the media room. He met Carlos's eyes.

"I, um ... I went to see Stevie Friday night, and, well ... we're together now."

"Oh, man, that's great! 'Bout time, too." Carlos reached down and clapped Dan on the shoulder. "I'm happy for you, *hermano.*"

"Thanks. I'm pretty happy about it myself." Dan blushed and grinned. "I took him to the meadow yesterday."

Carlos's eyebrows shot up. "You did? Whoa. Must be true love, bro, you never take anybody there." Carlos handed the level back down to Dan.

"Took you." Dan set the level back on the table.

"Hey, we're brothers, Danny," Carlos said as he climbed back down the ladder. "You gotta share that sort of thing with family."

"I know." Dan followed Carlos out into the foyer to start laying the new tiles. "Hey, Carlos?"

"Yeah?"

Dan laid a hand on Carlos's shoulder. "I don't know if I ever told you this, but I always thought of you like a brother, for real. You've been a good friend to me, and I just want you to know I appreciate it."

Carlos pulled Dan into a fierce hug. "You've been the same to me. I love you, man."

"Boys, boys! Get a room, huh?"

Dan blushed crimson at the sound of their co-worker's voice behind him. Carlos grinned and let go of Dan. "What, you jealous, Gary? I always knew you wanted me."

Gary made a face. "You're a sicko, Carlos. I'm telling Shawna I caught you groping Dan."

"Now who's the sicko? You don't grope your brother, but you do give him a hug when he needs it. Me and Danny, we're brothers."

"Dude, a guy doesn't hug another guy unless he's a fag or something." Gary narrowed his eyes at both of them. "Like I said. Couple of sickos."

Dan couldn't say a word. He felt frozen. Carlos gave him a worried look, then turned back to Gary with a rare flash of anger in his dark eyes.

"Listen up, *chilito*. My parents came here from a little town in Mexico. Down there, you tell your friends you love them. Families and friends take care of each other." He stalked up to Gary, who took a step back. "My parents taught me and my brothers and sisters to love each other and love our friends and to fucking say so. You could take a lesson from them, if you even have any friends. Asshole."

Gary turned red. "Whatever, dude." He gave them a dark look over his shoulder as he walked away.

"Fucking jackass," Carlos muttered. He turned concerned eyes to Dan. "You okay, bro?"

Dan studied his fingernails. "Is this what it's gonna be like?"

"Hey, don't listen to Gary, you know how he is. To him, anyone who's not a straight, white, Baptist man is less than human. Why you think he can't keep a girlfriend? They drop his skinny ass soon as they figure out he expects them to be his housekeeper and sex slave."

"Yeah, I know. He's not the only one o's gonna be like that, though." Dan stared at the bare wood under his feet. "I don't know if I can deal with all that shit just yet, Carlos."

"You wanna keep it quiet for a while?"

Dan looked back up. Carlos's eyes were calm and sympathetic. "Yeah, I think so."

"You know I won't tell anybody, bro. But how's Stevie feel about that?"

"We haven't really talked about it. I meant to, but ... well ..." Dan flushed and looked away.

"But you were busy," Carlos said, grinning. "Go, stud!"

"Shut up," Dan muttered.

Carlos laughed. "Seriously, *amigo*, if you wanna keep a low profile you better tell Stevie pretty soon. I'm thinking he's not the low-profile type."

"You got that right." Dan sighed. "I'm gonna talk to him tonight."

"Good." Carlos took out his pocket knife and started opening boxes of ceramic tile. "You guys moving in together?"

"Yeah, he's gonna move back in with me. He stayed over last night, matter of fact." Dan smiled, warmed by the memory of their lovemaking the night before, falling asleep in Stevie's arms, waking up, and doing it again. Leaving Stevie alone in bed, bare and flushed with sex, had been the hardest thing he'd ever had to do.

Carlos nudged his shoulder. "You're zoning out again, bro."

"Sorry." Dan dug in the toolbox for the trowel. "Just kind of wishing I could stay home with Stevie today."

"He's not working?"

"Nope." Dan started to tell Carlos about Roy, then stopped himself. It wasn't his story to tell. "John gave him the day off. Just, you know, because."

Carlos laughed. "John's a sucker for romance."

"He sure is. Now if only Joe was, too, maybe I could've gotten the day off."

"Danny, if you can get our boss to soften up that much, you let me know. I'd sure like a day at home with Shawna."

Dan grinned at him. "Y'all been married, what, eight years now? You ever gonna stop acting like newlyweds?"

"Eight and a half years," Carlos corrected. "And no, we're not."

Dan smiled as they got to work laying tile. He could picture himself and Stevie eight, ten, twenty years in the future, still together, still in love. It seemed crystal clear and inevitable. He concentrated on that vision while he worked, and eventually the nagging worry about Roy slipped to the back of his mind.

* * * * *

The morning passed quickly. Before Dan knew it, he and Carlos had nearly finished tiling the foyer, and it was past noon. Dan stood and stretched.

"Let's lay off for a while," he said. "Got a cramp in my back."

"Want some lunch?" Carlos asked, pushing to his feet.

"Yeah. Skipped breakfast this morning." Dan turned to rinse the trowel in the water bucket he kept handy.

"Yeah, the only thing you ate this morning was me."

Dan whirled around. Stevie stood there smiling, looking unbearably sexy in tight, hip-hugger jeans and the Princess shirt Dan had bought him. A strip of creamy skin showed between the jeans and t-shirt.

"Stevie!" Dan said. "What're you doing here?"

"Me and Shawna came over to eat with you guys." He rose on tiptoe to wind his arms around Dan's neck. "Missed you, Dan."

Dan pulled Stevie close. "Missed you, too." He tilted Stevie's face up and kissed him.

"Aw, y'all are so sweet together!"

Dan pulled away, blushing. "Hey, Shawna."

"Hey, Dan." She held out a Tupperware bowl. "Brownie? Stevie and I made them this morning."

"Thanks." Dan took a brownie and ate half of it in one bite. "Good."

"C'mon, let's go eat outside," Carlos said. "It's a nice day."

Stevie took Dan's hand as they followed Carlos and Shawna outside. He leaned close and rubbed his cheek on Dan's arm. "You don't mind me coming out to see you, do you, Dan?"

"'Course not. You're getting stir crazy all alone in that apartment, huh?"

"You know it." Stevie let out a deep sigh. "My nerves were all over the place. I feel so much better being here with you."

"Me, too." Dan squeezed Stevie's hand. "No sign of Roy?"

"Not a peep. Thank God."

Dan bit back the temptation to ask Stevie where to find Roy, so he could pound him into a pulp. He sat down on the blanket Shawna had spread out on the grass. Stevie plopped down next to him, thigh to thigh.

"So, Dan," Shawna said, "Stevie tells me he's moving back in with you."

"Yeah, that's the plan." Dan glanced around. Gary and some of the other guys sat around the picnic table on the other side of the backyard, looking his way and whispering together. He felt his face flush.

"I called John earlier," Stevie said. He unwrapped a sandwich and took a bite. "He said he'd help me move my stuff over tomorrow."

"Good. That's good." Dan shifted his knee away from Stevie's hand. He could practically feel the eyes of his co-workers on him.

"Yeah. He and Evan are gonna go with me to get my things after work. So they'll drive me home." Stevie laughed and leaned his head on Dan's shoulder. "Feels good to call it home, you know?"

A chorus of laughter sounded from the table where the other workers sat. Dan glanced over; all of them were staring at Stevie.

"Don't let them bother you, Danny," Carlos said. "Gary and his crew, they're not worth it."

Stevie stared at the group of sniggering men, then turned back to Dan. "What, did they say something?"

"Kind of," Dan said. "Earlier."

Stevie laughed. "You gotta learn not to let it get to you, Dan." He slid a hand up the inside of Dan's thigh. "C'mon, if they're gonna stare like idiots, let's give 'em something to look at."

"I don't ... I don't want to do that, Stevie," Dan said, pushing Stevie's hand away.

"Oh, come on." Stevie slipped an arm around Dan's waist. "It's fun to mess with people like that. It's almost too easy."

"Maybe so. But I have to work with these guys." Dan disentangled himself and pulled Stevie's hand out of his jeans pocket. "And I'd rather not have to listen to their teasing all day long."

Gary stood up and started swishing around the table. A couple of his group hooted and clapped. Others sat staring uncomfortably at the ground. Dan clenched his fists in his lap, torn between anger and embarrassment.

"God, what a bunch of assholes," Shawna muttered, shooting a dark look toward the picnic table.

Stevie laughed. "Hey, I can almost guarantee you at least one of them's jealous as hell right now and wishing he was me." He went up on his knees and kissed Dan's cheek.

"Hey, Dan!" Gary called from across the yard. "Didn't know you were queer! Can't you wait 'til you get home to get your ass plowed?"

Laughter from Gary's table, angry silence from Carlos and Shawna. Dan closed his eyes and forced himself to stay calm. He felt fury rising inside him and couldn't decide who he was angrier at: Gary, Stevie, or himself.

"Ignore him, baby," Stevie said in his ear. "He's nothing to us."

Stevie laid a hand on Dan's cheek, bent, and kissed his lips. For a heartbeat, Dan responded. Then jeers and catcalls cut through the fog of desire, and the anger and fear born of all his years in the closet exploded out of him.

"Stop it!" He pushed Stevie away and stood up. "Just fucking stop!"

Stevie stared up at him, blue eyes wide and shocked. "Dan ..."

"I told you, I have to work with these people! What the hell's so hard to understand? God, can't you keep your hands to yourself for five minutes?"

Dead silence. Even Gary didn't say a word. Stevie got slowly to his feet.

"Dan?" Stevie's voice was quiet and calm, but Dan could hear the hurt. "Are you ashamed of me?"

Dan wanted to say no, tell Stevie he loved him, that he was Dan's whole world. But his throat felt dry and tight, and he couldn't make a sound. He watched those big blue eyes fill with pure anguish, and he still couldn't make himself speak.

"I'm s-sorry, Dan," Stevie whispered. "I, I didn't mean ..." He bit his lip and backed away, tears spilling down his cheeks. "I ... I'm sorry."

Stevie turned and fled. He was gone before Dan could shake himself out of his paralysis. Shawna stopped him with a hand to his chest when he tried to follow Stevie.

"You've done plenty already," she said.

"But ... but I have to talk to him, Shawna. I have to tell him ..."

"Whatever you have to say, say it when you get home." Shawna's eyes flashed. "You'll just make it worse if you do it now, since evidently what those shitheads think is more important to you than Stevie's feelings."

She turned on her heel and hurried after Stevie. Dan stood there with his insides churning, feeling like the lowest possible form of life. He barely noticed when Carlos put a hand on his shoulder.

"Come on, *mi hermano*," Carlos said. "Let's go back inside, huh? You want me to bring your lunch?"

Dan shook his head. "No. I can't eat now." He felt numb. The first test of his commitment, and he'd failed miserably.

Dan let Carlos steer him into the media room. He sat down on a bit of plastic-draped carpet and covered his face with his hands. "God, Carlos. Fuck. Why the fuck did I do that?"

Carlos sat down next to him. "I think you were scared. You've been pretending to be straight all these years. I guess it's hard to stop pretending."

"That's no excuse for what I did, though. Gary and those others aren't worth the time of day, and I know it, but I let their stupid teasing upset me anyway."

"It's never easy to listen to that sort of shit."

"Then I should've ripped them all a new one instead of yelling at Stevie. He didn't deserve how I treated him." Dan met Carlos's eyes. "I love him, Carlos. I'm not ashamed of him. Why couldn't I tell him that?"

"Honestly? I don't know." Carlos slung an arm around Dan's shoulders. "But listen, it'll be okay. Shawna'll calm him down, then when you get home you can apologize. Then I think you and Stevie need to have a serious talk about this, so it doesn't happen again."

"Yeah." Dan managed a wan smile. "Thanks, Carlos. For not yelling at me."

"Hey, Shawna did a good enough job with that." Carlos stood and held down a hand to Dan. "Let's get back to work. Maybe we can finish early."

Dan let Carlos pull him to his feet. They gathered their supplies and went silently to work.

* * * * *

The afternoon lasted for eons. Dan did his best to keep his mind on his work, but he just couldn't. He kept seeing Stevie's face, blue eyes brimming with hurt. Pain he had caused, for no better reason than fear of being teased. Every time he thought of what he'd said to Stevie -- and what he should've said, but hadn't -- he felt sick. Nothing could ever be right again, he knew, until he could hold Stevie and kiss him and show him how much he loved him.

Carlos worked by Dan's side the whole time, and Dan was grateful for his silent but unwavering support. They managed to get everything done, thanks to Carlos keeping a watchful eye on Dan's work. By four o'clock they were ready to head home.

Throughout the afternoon, not one of their co-workers spoke to either of them. That was fine with Dan. He didn't want to deal with the pity he saw on some faces any more than he wanted to deal with the disgust on others. When Joe stopped him on the way to Carlos's pick-up, it was all he could do to keep himself from screaming.

"Everything's done, Joe." He kept his voice as calm as he could. "And I've got someplace to be."

"This won't take a minute." Joe hooked his thumbs in his belt and stared up at Dan with grim determination. "I just wanted to tell you, I talked to Gary and some of those other boys. They won't be bothering you again. If they do, you let me know, and their asses are fired. I told 'em so, too. Everybody on my team plays nice, or they don't play."

Dan forced a smile. Joe was a tough, no-nonsense boss, but he was always fair. He didn't tolerate harassment or discrimination of any sort. He and Dan would never be friends, but he was a good person to have on your side.

"Thanks, Joe," Dan said.

"See you tomorrow." Joe gave him a curt nod and hurried away.

The ride back home seemed to take forever. Dan felt an overwhelming sense of urgency that had him literally on the edge of his seat, chewing his thumbnail and frowning out the window. He was out of the truck almost before Carlos had it parked.

"Good luck, *amigo*," Carlos said as he exited the stairwell on the second floor.

"Thanks, Carlos. See you in the morning."

Carlos squeezed his arm, turned and headed down the hall. Dan continued up to his floor.

His hands shook when he unlocked the door. "Stevie? I'm home. I have to talk to you, I'm really sorry about today ..."

He trailed off when he saw the empty living room. The apartment was utterly silent. Apprehension made his pulse speed up.

"Stevie?" He peered into the kitchen. Empty.

He ran into the bedroom, hoping that Stevie was simply asleep and didn't hear him come in. But the bedroom was as empty as the rest of the place.

Something white lay in the middle of the neatly made bed. Dan flipped the light on and went to look. It was a piece of paper, folded over, with his name written in big, shaky letters across the outside. He snatched it up and opened it. What he saw made his heart thud painfully against his ribs.

"Dear Dan," the note read. "I'm sorry, but I can't stay with you. I'm just not good enough. I know that now. So I'm going away. Maybe back to Aspen, I don't know. Please don't hate me, I never meant to hurt you. I hope you find someone who can be what you want. I'm sorry I couldn't be. I'll always love you. Stevie."

Dan closed his eyes, fighting panic. Stevie couldn't be gone. He just couldn't.

"Shawna," Dan mumbled to himself. "Maybe he changed his mind, maybe he went to see Shawna."

He raced into the kitchen and dialed Carlos and Shawna's apartment. Shawna picked up on the second ring.

"Hello?"

"Hey, Shawna, it's Dan. Is Stevie over there?"

"No, he's not. I left him at your place about, oh, three hours ago, after I thought he'd settled down enough to be alone." The reproach in her voice was restrained, but unmistakable. "What, are you saying he's not there?"

"No. No, he ... he left a note ... but I was hoping he'd changed his mind, that maybe ..." Dan's shaking voice trailed off.

"Oh, my God," Shawna said after a silent moment. "You mean he left? For good?"

"I, I think he did."

"Oh, Dan, no! Shit, I knew I should've stayed with him, I knew it! But, but I had to pick the kids up, oh, God, I should've called my sister or someone to do that, Stevie needed me, and I left him alone! Oh, God, Dan, I'm so sorry!"

"Shawna, I think we both know there's no one to blame but me." Dan stopped, fighting back tears.

"Dan, sweetie, why don't you come down here? Or let me come up there, I could ..."

"No," Dan interrupted. "No, thanks, I just ... I need to be alone right now."

"Well ... okay. But please, Dan, call us if you need us, okay? Any time."

"Yeah, I will. Thanks, Shawna."

The phone fell from Dan's hand as he clicked it off. He sat down on the kitchen floor and sobbed, clutching Stevie's note to his chest. Even after the tears finally tapered off, he stayed there for a long time.

CHAPTER FOURTEEN

Stevie was dreaming.

He knew it was only a dream. But he didn't care. He savored every second of it. Because in his dream, things were different. In his dream, Dan came home and took him in his arms and kissed him, and they made love for hours and everything was fine. He much preferred the dream to what had actually happened.

Of course, no dream can last forever. Eventually, Stevie felt himself floating toward wakefulness. He fought it as hard as he could, clinging to dream-Dan and crying the tears that never would come when he was awake. But it was no good. The comfort of his dream gave way to harsh reality all too soon, and Stevie lay blinking up at the water-stained ceiling of his little room.

He shivered and pulled the threadbare blanket tighter around himself. December in the mountains was cold, and the heat in this old building was less than reliable. And he wasn't allowed clothes anymore, not after he almost got away that one time.

The headlights of the cars passing by outside made shifting patterns of light and shadow on the bare walls. Traffic was heavy, too heavy for a week night. Must be Friday, or maybe Saturday. Always busy nights. He sighed, rubbed his eyes, and rolled over to look at the clock. Almost seven. Someone would be in to get him soon.

Sure enough, a key rattled in the door, and it squealed open. He blinked against the sudden brightness as the overhead light flickered on. A tall, dark-skinned young man stood in the doorway, scowling at him. "C'mon, pretty boy. Boss says you got a customer waiting already. I gotta get you washed up."

Stevie stood without a word. The boy -- Zeke, that was his name -- handed him a robe. He shrugged it on and followed Zeke down the hall to the bathroom.

Two more boys were waiting in the big, green-tiled room. One of them stood grinning ear to ear and twirling a razor between his fingers. Stevie's stomach lurched.

"Hey, Sunshine," the boy with the razor said. "Ready to get all dolled up?"

"Shut up, Hal," Zeke growled. "Let's just get this done. I got lots to do."

Hal shook his head. "Zeke, you gotta learn to enjoy found pleasures, my man."

"You get off on shaving this kid, fine. But I don't." Zeke pushed past Hal and turned the shower on. "Okay, Sunshine. In. Make sure you wash good, I ain't doing it for you this time."

Stevie let the robe fall to the floor and stepped into the shower. The three boys stood silently watching him while he soaped up and shampooed his hair. They never left him alone anymore, except when he slept.

Stevie closed his eyes and ducked his head under the lukewarm water, rinsing the shampoo out. It smelled vaguely medicinal. He missed Dan's shampoo, with its soft, green scent. He missed Dan. More than a month had passed, but the black hole inside him had only grown bigger.

It had all happened so fast. Dan's public rejection had cut deep, but he'd eventually realized that it was fear making Dan react that way. He knew Dan would've come home and folded him into those strong arms and said he was sorry. Stevie had already forgiven him. He would have apologized for not listening to what Dan was trying to tell him, and they'd have made love, and everything would have been all right again. They could have worked it out.

When he'd heard the door open, he'd thought it was Dan, coming home early. He'd run to greet him. But Dan wasn't there.

He'd tried to get away, of course. But Roy had brought enforcers, and Stevie didn't stand a chance. The hope that Dan would suspect Roy had taken him was dashed when Roy packed all his things to take with them, then made him write that damned note. He wouldn't have done it, but Roy threatened Dan with the most horrible tortures if he didn't. He knew Roy would do it. And he'd rather have Dan safe, even if it meant he never saw him again and that Dan cursed his name forever.

So he wrote the note, and Roy took him back to his own private hell.

He'd almost escaped once, the first week. After that, Roy took his clothes and kept him locked in his second-floor room in the ancient hotel Roy used for his business. The other boys brought him his meals and escorted him to the bathroom to bathe and use the toilet. This arrangement made no one happy except Roy. Roy was happy because the hundred an hour he managed to con men into paying for Stevie netted him hundreds of dollars a night. Stevie hadn't seen a cent of it. He was no more than a slave now.

Stevie was yanked abruptly out of his thoughts when Zeke turned the water off and pulled him out of the shower. "Come on, we ain't got all damn night. Now lie down and spread 'em. We gotta shave you."

Stevie swallowed against the bile rising in his throat. He hated being shaved. It nearly always meant a john who wanted him to play young and submissive, which usually meant pain. That happened way more often now than it used to. The men Roy sent him invariably smelled of money and arrogance, but he'd learned the hard way that they liked a more sordid brand of pleasure than their blue-collar counterparts.

"Move it, Sunshine." Hal licked the handle of the razor he held. His amber eyes gleamed.

Stevie stared at his bare feet. "Can I have a towel? To lie on? The floor's cold."

Hal started to say no, but Zeke cut him off. "David," he said, addressing the third boy who stood wide-eyed and silent against the wall, "put a towel down here, and then fill up that bucket with water."

Hal gave Zeke a murderous look, but didn't dare say anything. Zeke was Roy's number-one enforcer and more than capable of breaking Hal in half if he wanted. David edged forward and spread a big, faded blue towel on the floor. He looked ready to bolt.

"Okay, there's your towel," Zeke said. "So quit stalling and get your skinny ass the fuck on the floor. Now."

Stevie lowered himself to the floor and sat there for a second, gathering his courage. Zeke kicked him in the chest, sending him tumbling backward. His head hit the floor with an audible crack. Something was wound tightly around his wrists. A tugging at his arms told him they'd tied his wrists to the radiator.

Zeke leaned over and frowned at Stevie. "I'm about done messing with you, pretty boy." He hooked an arm under Stevie's left knee and signaled David to do the same with the other one. They pulled his legs up and apart. "You better start behaving, hear me? You just fucking remember you brought this on yourself. You could be taking care of all this shit yourself, but no, you had to be stubborn and tell Roy you wouldn't do it. Dumbass."

Stevie closed his eyes. He blocked out Zeke's voice, ignored the pain in his shoulders and the scrape of the razor over his balls, and let his mind float away. When Hal unzipped his jeans and rubbed off against Stevie's newly shorn skin, he kept his eyes shut and pretended it was Dan. Zeke's complaints about having to wash him again barely registered.

They led him back to his room, docile as a sheep, still lost in his memories of Dan. He didn't resist when they slipped a white lace baby-doll dress on him, or when David sat him down on the edge of the bed to make up his face. When David held a mirror up for him to see, over Zeke's impatient objections, Stevie saw nothing there that he recognized. The painted red lips, the white skin, and especially those dead, dead eyes. That wasn't him.

He turned away without a word.

* * * * *

"Goddammit. Fucking psycho bastard. Last time I let one of those sick fucks in here, goddammit. Gonna lose money on this. People find out that hundred-an-hour whore's all beat up, they ain't gonna want to pay. Fuck."

Stevie lay on his stomach, the lace dress wadded underneath him, and listened to Roy cursing while he cleaned the blood off of Stevie's thighs and buttocks. It should've hurt, but it didn't. It had sure as hell hurt when the man's thick leather belt cut into his skin. At first, anyway. After the first few blows, Stevie hardly felt it anymore.

This one hadn't wanted to fuck him. He'd ordered Stevie to pull his dress up and spread his legs, then spent several minutes fondling him, cooing to him about what a pretty little boy he was. He'd probed briefly inside Stevie with one blunt finger before tearing the dress off and making him turn over. The remainder of the hour had been spent alternately whipping Stevie and coating his back with semen.

"Dumb shit. Goddammit. See how he fucking likes it when his business burns to the goddamn ground. See how he makes money then. Asshole." Roy stood and stretched. "Well, I reckon that's 'bout as good as it gets. Get up, boy, let's have a look at you."

Stevie rolled over and stood up on shaky legs. Roy circled him with a critical eye. "You'll do. Now get back on that bed, on all fours."

Stevie did as he was told. He didn't even flinch when Roy pushed a big square pillow under his chest, yanked his arms behind his back, and tied his wrists together, then cuffed a spreader bar to his ankles. A few months ago, he would've panicked. Now, he was too dead inside to care.

"He ain't gonna damage you none," Roy said. "I'm 'bout sick of that shit. I told him if there's a mark on you that wasn't there when he went in, I'll break every bone in his goddamn body. Now you just stay right there, and don't you move a fuckin' muscle. I'm goin' to get him."

Roy's footsteps sounded across the room and out. The door clicked shut. Stevie waited. Minutes later, he heard the door open and close again. Slow footfalls toward the bed, cold hands on his thighs. He squeezed his eyes shut and started to retreat into his mind.

"Hello, Stevie."

Stevie's eyes flew open. Jesse. It was Jesse.

"You know, I really like seeing you like this." Jesse ran his palm over the raw cuts. "Yeah, I like it a lot. A whore ought to look like a whore, and you sure as fuck do right now."

"How'd you know, Jesse?" Stevie was amazed by how strong and clear his voice was. "How'd you know I worked for Roy?"

Jesse was silent for a minute, rolling Stevie's balls between his fingers. "I used to rent from him now and then. Just occasionally, you know, not all the time or anything. I used to hear some of the boys talking about this kid Roy had, real pretty kid. They called him Sunshine. Never saw him. Never was much interested, to tell you the truth. I don't rent for a pretty face, I rent for something I can fuck however I want and not have to talk to after."

Jesse gave Stevie's balls a hard squeeze. Stevie forced himself to not react.

"Anyway," Jesse continued, "I went downtown for some quick head awhile after we started dating, and all the boys were talking about how Sunshine had gone missing. They were scared because they thought one of his johns had killed him. I didn't put two and two together until after you broke up with me for that fucking gorilla. After that, it occurred to me that the way the boys described Sunshine sounded an awful lot like you. And the timing? Sunshine missing, Stevie suddenly popping up, no explanation of where you came from or anything? Way too convenient to be a coincidence. Especially after I figured out what a fucking slut you are, doing that slack-jawed moron behind my back. So, I asked around. Got a picture from one of the boys. And there you go."

Stevie clenched his jaw. Anger stirred inside him for the first time in weeks, but it wasn't enough to overcome the lassitude he'd lived in since his failed escape attempt. When Jesse walked around the bed and into Stevie's field of vision, Stevie met his triumphant smirk with a complete lack of expression.

"So," Jesse said. "How's it feel, Stevie? Having me for a customer? 'Cause I like it. I like getting to treat you like the whore you are."

Stevie turned his face away. "Just do it."

Jesse grabbed a handful of Stevie's hair and yanked his head up. "You think I want to fuck you? Hell, no. I'm not sticking my dick in anything that filthy. Your ass is getting this --" He brandished an enormous steel vibrator. "-- and I get to watch your face when I tell you I'm the one who told Roy where to find you." He leaned down, nose to nose with Stevie, gray eyes feverish. "I'm the reason you're here instead of with that fucking redneck. What do you think about that, huh?"

Stevie managed a bitter smile. The movement felt unfamiliar and strange.

"I knew that, you stupid fuck," he heard himself say. "Now just shut up and get it over with."

Jesse's eyes narrowed. He drew back the hand that wasn't clenched in Stevie's hair, and Stevie had a split second to mentally brace himself before the vibrator smashed into his jaw. His vision blurred, and he tasted blood. The pain seemed a remote thing, unconnected with him.

"That's gonna cost you a kneecap." His voice sounded weak and slurred. "You don't mess with Roy's boys. Dumb shit."

Jesse's face turned bright red. Stevie started laughing. He'd robbed Jesse of his ability to gloat, and it was just too funny.

"Shut up, you fucking little whore!" Jesse shouted. "That's all you are, is a whore! That's all you ever were!"

Jesse dragged Stevie to his knees by the hair. Stevie laughed harder. He couldn't seem to stop. Jesse's helpless rage felt like a vindication of sorts for all he'd suffered over the past month.

"We could've had something, Stevie," Jesse hissed. His face was inches from Stevie's, hard and dark with fury. "You threw it all away, for a dumb fuck who didn't even want you."

Stevie stared right into Jesse's eyes. "You were never anything but a good lay to me, Jesse. Me and Dan? That was love. Now just do what the fuck you paid for and get out." He spat a mouthful of blood in Jesse's face.

Jesse scrambled backward, scrubbing at his eyes. Stevie started laughing again, so hard he could barely breathe. He knew what was coming, but he didn't care. It would be worth it for the look on Jesse's face right then. He kept right on laughing when Jesse swung the metal vibrator hard at his head. It impacted the side of his skull with a thunk. A thin, bright pain stabbed through Stevie's head. He heard footsteps, the door opening and slamming closed again. He smiled to himself as he fell forward and drifted into unconsciousness.

CHAPTER FIFTEEN

"So, Bob, what's ahead for the weather this weekend?"

"Well, Mitzi, it looks like a nice weekend coming up. Daytime highs will only reach into the mid-thirties, but it'll be nice and sunny with negligible wind chill. Looking at the extended forecast ..."

Dan clicked the TV off. He'd turned it on in the first place to drown out the memories that threatened to overwhelm him in even the briefest moments of silence. But every image, every conversation, only made it worse. Everything made him think of Stevie.

He got up off the couch and felt his way through his darkened apartment to the window seat. He'd never paid much attention to that spot before. Now, it comforted him. When he curled up on the padded seat and gazed out at the winter night, he felt somehow connected to Stevie.

Stevie. Just thinking his name made Dan's throat constrict, even after more than a month without him. He'd tried being angry with Stevie for leaving without giving them a chance, but he couldn't do it. What had happened was his own fault, no one else's. He couldn't blame Stevie for going. All he could do now was miss him, hope he was happy, and try to move on.

He hadn't had much luck with that so far. Dan could feel himself sinking deeper each day into a black depression. His performance at work had fallen off to the point where Joe had put him on leave. He had six weeks, Joe said, to get his shit together, or he was fired. He couldn't bring himself to care. He'd stopped talking to his friends, and for the last two weeks he hadn't left his apartment at all, not even to buy groceries.

Without Stevie, nothing seemed to matter.

Carlos and Shawna weren't at all shy about using their key to Dan's apartment. He figured that was the only reason he hadn't starved to death yet. He remained obstinately silent, never telling them how he felt, but he was grateful for their staunch friendship.

Shawna had called John and Evan and told them what happened. They'd come over -- at John's insistence, Dan was sure -- and told him that they were so sorry, to call them if he needed anything. They weren't angry with Stevie for leaving without telling them, Dan was relieved to hear. It would've killed him for John and Evan to be angry at Stevie because of him. Dan thanked them, accepted John's tearful hug and Evan's solemn handshake, and hadn't spoken to them since. Part of him felt bad about how he was neglecting the people he cared about, who he knew cared about him as well. But he just couldn't find the energy to interact anymore. He hoped his friends would understand and forgive him.

He leaned his head against the window. The icy glass frosted with his breath. He gazed up at the sky and wondered where under all that starry expanse Stevie was and what he was doing.

A knock sounded on the door. He ignored it. After a few seconds there was a louder knock, and this time it was followed by Melina's voice. "Dan! I know you're there, let me in!"

The unusual note of urgency in her voice convinced Dan to get up and open the door. She brushed past him, flipping the light on as she went.

"Hi, Melina." Dan shut the door and turned to face Melina, squinting in the light.

"I saw him."

Dan frowned. "Who?"

Melina came to Dan and took his hands. Her eyes glinted with a combination of discovery and fear. "Stevie. I saw Stevie."

Dan stared at her. "You ... what? Are you sure?"

"Positive." She tugged Dan to the couch. They sat down side by side. "I mean it was only for a minute, but I got a good look at his face. I know it was him."

The blood roared in Dan's ears. He felt weak and dizzy. "Where?"

"Downtown. I'd been to Malaprop's and was heading across town to Aaron's place. So I was stopped at a red light, and I saw these guys getting out of a big car in front of an old building just up the street. There were two of them helping another one walk, it looked like. And the guy they were helping turned toward me for a minute, and ... and it was Stevie. He was right there in my headlights. It was him."

"Oh. Oh." Dan stared helplessly at Melina. Everything felt unreal and off-kilter. "Stevie. Oh."

"Dan, something's wrong. He had bruises on his face, and he looked ... I don't know. He looked so beaten down." She squeezed his hand. "I think he's in some sort of trouble."

In a blinding flash, Dan knew. His stomach dropped into his shoes. "Oh, my God. Roy."

Melina furrowed her brow at him. "Who's Roy?"

Dan sat silent for a moment, wondering how much to tell her. And decided the hell with it, Stevie's safety was far more important than his reputation. He took a deep breath.

"Roy was Stevie's pimp, Melina."

"What? You mean Stevie ..."

"Yeah," Dan interrupted. "But that was before. He hasn't done that in months. He was done with that life. But the night before I ... before he left, he said Roy had gone to Rainbow Books looking for him. That's why he was moving in with me."

All the color drained from Melina's face. "Oh, shit. Stevie didn't really leave you at all, did he? That Roy person took him."

"I think so." Dan swallowed, fighting a growing fear. "And I've got this feeling Jesse's the one who told him where to find Stevie."

"Oh, come on. I know he can be a real jackass sometimes, but surely to God he wouldn't do anything that awful."

"I hope not. But I can't figure it out otherwise. He knows where I live. He knew where Stevie lived and where he worked.

And I saw him downtown the day after Stevie broke up with him, talking to some rough-looking kid."

"So, you think Stevie told Jesse about his past?"

"No, he never did."

Melina frowned. "Well, then, how the hell did he know?"

Dan shook his head. "I don't know. It doesn't matter anyhow, not now. We gotta get Stevie out of there."

"Yeah. Yeah, we do." Melina jumped up. "I'll call the police."

Dan sat and chewed his fingernails while Melina dialed the police department and talked her way patiently through the layers of underlings until someone finally put her through to a detective. He got up and wandered over to the window. Melina's voice grew increasingly louder and more frustrated. Finally she slammed the phone down with a clang.

"Goddammit!" She plopped down on the couch again and pressed both palms to her eyes. "Stupid jerks!"

Dan turned and stared solemnly down at her. "They didn't believe you?"

"They said that they couldn't start arresting people just because I thought they looked suspicious. I said what about Stevie's bruises, what about him being here at all when he'd said he was leaving, what about Roy looking for him before? They said hookers always have bruises and that Stevie had obviously gone back to hustling and didn't want us to know." She sighed. "So what now?"

Dan turned again, staring out at the cold December night. He felt utterly helpless. He'd have given anything to hold Stevie right then. Hold him and kiss him and stroke his hair, touch that soft, soft skin. It made him feel cold inside to think of the abuse he'd probably suffered at the hands of his "customers."

Customers.

"Oh, hell," Dan said. "That's it."

Melina turned a puzzled look to him. "What's what?"

Dan jumped up and starting looking for his wallet and keys, which he hadn't touched in two weeks. "Melina, where was that building? Can you show me?"

"Sure. But what ..." Melina's eyes widened. "Dan, you're not thinking of barging in and trying to find him, are you? We don't even know if he's still there!"

"That wasn't exactly what I had in mind." Dan finally found his wallet under a pile of mail in the corner. He stuck it in his back pocket and continued the search for his keys.

"Then what did you have in mind?"

Dan fished the key ring out of the kitchen drawer where it had somehow ended up and turned to Melina with a grim smile. "I'm gonna pretend to be a customer."

Melina stood up. "Oh, my God, Dan, that's brilliant. You ask for Stevie; Roy takes you right to him."

Dan nodded as they pulled their jackets on. "Roy's never seen me. Least I hope not. So he wouldn't have any reason to think I wasn't a paying customer."

"What if he has seen you, Dan? What if he recognizes you?" Melina pulled the door open, and they headed outside. She looked worried.

"I don't know." Dan locked the door, frowning in thought. "I'll think of something."

Dan started toward the stairs. Melina stopped him with a hand on his arm. "Promise you'll be careful, okay? Promise you'll keep your eyes open and get out of there if it looks like he's not falling for it."

"I promise," Dan lied.

Melina smiled at him, leaned over, and kissed his cheek. "Let's go."

* * * * *

Melina had no trouble finding the old corner building where she'd seen Stevie. Dan glanced at it as he drove slowly by. Ancient and dilapidated, mossy brick with dull gray paint peeling off the window frames and narrow front door. It looked thoroughly seedy, but not abandoned. Lights in several of the small, barred windows told him it was definitely occupied.

"Okay, here's the plan." He pulled into an empty parking space a couple of blocks up the street, in the neon glow of a busy dance club. "I'm gonna go in and ask for Roy and tell him I want to ... that I want to rent Stevie." Just saying those words put a bad taste in Dan's mouth. He ignored it and pushed on. "I'm sure he'll take me to him. From what Stevie's told me, Roy sounds like a greedy bastard. I don't think he'll turn down the chance to make money. And soon as I find Stevie, and the coast is clear, I'm taking him out of there."

"I hope you know what you're doing, Dan." Melina sat twisting her hands together in her lap, glancing nervously out at the street, which still teemed with people at not quite midnight on a Friday.

"You got any better ideas, I'm listening. But I can't leave Stevie there. I have to do something."

Melina sighed. "No, I can't think of anything else. Dammit."

"Okay." Dan unbuckled his seatbelt and grasped Melina's hand. "You stay here. Lock the doors and keep the keys to the Jeep, in case you have to leave. This isn't the best part of town. And keep your cell phone on. I've got mine, and I'll try and call you if I run into any trouble."

"You be careful, Dan." She pulled him into a hug.

"I will, don't worry." He patted Melina's back, pulled away, and stepped out into the street.

The people jostling him on all sides were a varied lot. Goth kids, hippies, street people, business types with a purposeful stride and eyes fixed on the grubby sidewalk. This part of town was on the cusp of the revitalization movement. A few renovated businesses attracted slumming tourists, but mostly it was where locals came to indulge their favorite vices. A place where no one would notice or care what you did.

Dan stood outside and watched the men entering and leaving the old building. Most didn't seem any different from himself, just regular guys in jeans and t-shirts. A few had that slick, polished look that screamed money. Dan took a deep breath and headed resolutely for the door.

The front door opened onto a narrow, dimly lit hallway, unaccountably painted a dull orange. A small room opened to his right. In it, several men sat on cracked leather chairs or the worn sofa, some alone and obviously waiting, others with boys of questionable legality on their laps. A boy with burnished-copper skin and a single long, coal-black braid stood up from his spot between two middle-aged men and walked over to Dan.

"You need something, mister?" The boy's voice was gruff and suspicious. "This here's a private party."

Dan gave him what he hoped was a winning smile. "I'm looking for Roy."

The boy's black eyes narrowed. "Don't know no Roy."

"Yeah, you do." Dan leaned toward the boy. His heart pounded so hard he could hear it. He hoped no one else could. "I want Sunshine. Heard you gotta talk to Roy for that."

The young man gave Dan a sharp look. Dan held his breath and hoped he hadn't blown his chance. He nearly collapsed from relief when the boy nodded and headed into the hall, beckoning Dan to follow. Evidently his instinct about having to go through Roy to get to Stevie had been correct.

"Hey, Kane! Get back here, boy, we already paid!"

Dan's guide turned toward the man who'd shouted at him. "I'll be right back, okay? He's here to see Roy, I gotta take him." He whirled back around, braid swinging. "Come on, mister. I can't keep my customers waiting long."

Dan followed Kane to the end of the hall. Kane knocked on the last door on the left.

"What?" called a gravely voice from inside.

"Customer to see you, Roy," Kane said. "Says he wants Sunshine."

Silence for a moment. Then the door scraped open and a small, wiry, hard-looking man stood staring up at Dan with eyes sharp as lasers. Kane turned and stalked back to the front room without a word.

"Sunshine ain't seein' nobody else tonight," Roy said.

"Why not?" Dan congratulated himself on not sounding as anxious as he felt.

"Some dumbass got too rough earlier. Doc said he had to rest tonight. He'll be back on the job tomorrow night, you come back then. A hundred an hour, in advance."

Dan swallowed his panic and tried to act normal. "I don't wanna wait. I want him right now."

Roy scowled. "Well, mister, you ain't got much choice. 'Less you want one of the other boys. I got some just as good and a couple almost as pretty."

"No. Sunshine's the one I want. I don't care if he's not feeling good." *Please*, Dan thought, *please*.

Roy's expression turned thunderous. "Mister, you better turn your ass right around and get the fuck out of my place 'fore I get pissed off. I said Sunshine ain't seein' nobody else tonight, and my word is fuckin' law around here. Got that?"

"But ..."

"But nothin'. You come back tomorrow before seven, you can have Sunshine. Right now, if none of my other boys are good enough for you, you'd best get out."

Roy slammed the door shut. Dan stood there for a minute, shaking with rage and desperation. He had to force himself to turn away and walk back out the door without Stevie.

He walked back to the Jeep, fear for Stevie making his feet feel like lead. Melina unlocked the door for him and frowned as he climbed in.

"What happened? Wasn't he there?"

"He's there, someplace. I saw Roy, and he said Stevie wasn't seeing anybody tonight. Said somebody had got too rough with him earlier." Dan leaned his head on the steering wheel. "He's hurt, Melina. Some shithead hurt him, and I can't do anything about it. I'd just go right in and take him, if I knew where he was, but I don't. God, I fucking hate this."

Melina slid an arm around Dan's shoulders. "We'll think of something else, Dan. We're not giving up."

"Hell, no, we're not." Dan raised his head again. "Roy said I could see Stevie tomorrow night. I'm going back, then."

"I'll come with you."

"No, I'm not taking you in that place; it's too dangerous. I'm going alone."

"No, Dan, please don't." Her green eyes pleaded with him. "What if you need help to get him out? If you won't let me go with you, get Carlos. He can fight if he has to."

Dan started to protest, then stopped. She was right. He had no idea how badly Stevie was hurt, or how difficult it might be to get him out. He nodded. "Okay. I'll talk to Carlos in the morning."

"Good." Melina patted Dan's knee. "We'll get Stevie out of there, Dan. And as soon as we do, we're calling the police again and shut that damn place down."

Dan nodded and tried to smile. He glanced over his shoulder at the building where Stevie lay somewhere, alone and injured. It took every ounce of strength he had to drive away. Soon, Stevie, he silently promised. Soon.

* * * * *

Saturday morning dawned bright, cold, and cloudless. Dan watched the sky lighten from the window seat, where he'd spent an endless, sleepless night staring into the darkness. He could feel Stevie out there. Every cell in his body ached to go to that building and tear the place apart, with his bare hands if he had to, to find Stevie.

After the sun peeked over the treetops, he got up with a deep sigh and went to call Carlos. Ten minutes later, Carlos was sitting at Dan's kitchen table, sipping coffee and listening to Dan tell the whole story of how he'd met Stevie, and what had really happened when he left. Carlos absorbed the news with his usual unflappable calm.

"Shit." Carlos frowned thoughtfully at his coffee. "This Roy guy sounds pretty bad. How you gonna get Stevie out of there?"

"I'm gonna pretend to be a customer. I went there last night, and I saw Roy. He told me Stevie was hurt and not seeing anybody, and to come back tonight before seven." Dan cupped his coffee mug in both hands and took a sip. "Hardest thing I ever had to do, walking away from there knowing Stevie was in there someplace, hurt and needing help."

Carlos stared at him, dark eyes very serious. "Danny, this is gonna be dangerous. Let me come with you, *hermano*. In case someone tries to stop you."

Dan gave him an anemic smile. "I was sort of hoping you would. Melina wanted to go, but it's a pretty rough part of town, and I didn't like putting her in danger. So she said I should ask you."

"Melina's tougher than she looks. She could probably handle herself just fine. But you take a woman in a place like that, I'm thinking it's gonna draw attention you don't want. I'm guessing this is an all-boy operation?"

"Yeah. And you're right -- a woman would draw a lot of attention." Dan leaned forward on his elbows. "So are you okay with this?"

"I'm in, bro."

"What about Shawna? You think she'll be upset?"

Carlos smiled. "Nope. She'll understand that it's the right thing to do. And she knows I can take care of myself."

"Good. I wouldn't upset Shawna for anything." Dan stared solemnly at Carlos. "I'll come to your place around six, okay?"

"Sounds good." They both stood. Carlos held out his hand. "*Hermanos*, Dan. Brothers."

"Always." They clasped hand in hand, and Dan felt stronger.

* * * * *

The day dragged. By the time six o'clock arrived, Dan felt he'd lived a whole hellish millennium. It couldn't possibly have been less than half a day. When he knocked on Carlos and Shawna's door, he thought surely he'd aged so much they wouldn't recognize him.

After a solemn, whispered good-bye between Carlos and Shawna, the two men climbed into Dan's Jeep and set off. The mood was tense and grim, and they rode in silence. Dan parked as close as he could get this time, about half a block up the street.

"So what's the plan?" Carlos asked as they started up the sidewalk.

"I want to go get Stevie together, if we can. I don't know how bad he's hurt, or how far he can get without help. So what I figured is, I'd tell Roy we ... well, that we both ... um ..." Dan glanced uncomfortably over at Carlos.

Carlos nodded. "I get it. Yeah, that's probably a good idea. You think they'll want extra?"

"Shit, I hadn't thought of that. Roy said it was a hundred an hour, in advance. But that was just for one, I don't know how they work it with two." Dan bit his lip. "How much you got on you? I've got about a hundred and fifty."

"Let's see. I've probably got seventy-five or so. Think that'll be enough?"

"It'd better be."

They came to a halt in front of the peeling front door of Roy's whorehouse. Dan laid a hand on Carlos's shoulder. "Carlos, you sure you want to help me? Like you said, it might be dangerous. And now you're probably gonna lose money, too."

"The money's nothing. This is Stevie's life we're talking about here." Carlos gripped Dan's hand. "Let's do this, *hermano.*"

"Yeah. Okay." Dan squared his shoulders and opened the door.

The front room looked much the same as it had the night before. Dan recognized several of the boys and a couple of the customers as well. The boy with the braid -- Kane, Dan remembered -- spotted him, smiled, and came walking over.

"Back already?" the young man said.

"Didn't get to see Sunshine last night. Roy said he wasn't seeing anybody. So I came back." Dan managed a shaky smile.

"Brought a friend, too, huh?" Kane's eyes went soft, his mouth curving into a seductive smile. He draped an arm over Carlos's shoulder. "What about you let me take care of you while your friend's busy?"

Carlos managed to look blankly ignorant. "*No hablo inglés,*" he said, shrugging apologetically.

"Sorry, but he doesn't like to play. He just wants to watch." Dan hooked his arm through Carlos's elbow.

"Too bad." Kane moved his arm, letting his dark eyes linger. "Guess you wanna talk to Roy?"

"Yeah," Dan said.

"All right, come on."

They followed Kane's swinging braid down the hall. Carlos leaned close, squeezing Dan's arm. "Good save, *amigo*. And thanks."

"No problem."

Roy's door opened just as the boy was about to knock. Roy grinned when he saw Dan, steely eyes flicking between him and Carlos. "Figured you'd be back. Double for two." He smacked Kane hard on the cheek. "Get the fuck back there."

The boy flinched away from Roy's raised hand, and fled back to the front room.

"He's only watching," Dan said, nodding toward Carlos. "Don't we get a discount for that?"

"How the hell do I know he's only watchin'? All I got's your word, 'less I go watch myself, and I don't wanna. Two hundred, or get the fuck out."

Dan and Carlos glanced at each other. They pulled out their wallets and silently counted out two hundred dollars. Roy took it, his whole face lit with greed. Dan fought hard against the urge to pound him right through the floor. Carlos's firm grip on his arm grounded him and kept him focused on what was important: Stevie. He had to stay calm and not lose his cool if they were to get Stevie out of there.

"All right, you boys can wait in the front room while I get 'im ready. Won't be long." Roy stuck the wad of cash in his shirt pocket, turned, and headed up the narrow back stairs across the hall from his office.

Carlos pulled Dan's arm. "Come on, Danny."

Dan let Carlos lead him toward the front room. His pulse thudded in his temples, and every muscle in his body sang with tension.

"Coming, Stevie," he whispered. "I'm coming."

CHAPTER SIXTEEN

The slap was hard enough to sting, but not hard enough to leave more than a faint red mark. Stevie laid a hand over the palm-shaped warmth on his cheek and bit back a laugh. He took a strange, distant sort of pleasure in Roy's frustration. He didn't even mind the way his lingering headache flared when Roy hit him.

"Goddammit, boy," Roy growled. "Didn't I tell you to clean up between customers? Who the hell wants to fuck a kid with somebody else's come all over him?"

"Clean up how, Roy?" Stevie mumbled. "My tongue? I'm not that flexible."

Roy's face darkened with anger. Stevie let out a giggle as Roy realized he was right. The tiny room didn't even have a sink, and Roy hadn't designated anyone to be Stevie's bath guard for the night. Roy turned and stalked out of the room. He returned a couple of minutes later with a wet washcloth and a towel.

"There," Roy said, throwing both onto the bed. "Wash off, and be quick about it. You got two waitin' for you downstairs."

Stevie picked up the cold washcloth and swabbed off the evidence of his last trick. He was glad to be rid of the reminder. The man hadn't wanted anything but to watch Stevie masturbate, so it should've been easy. But the only way Stevie could manage it was to think of Dan. And thinking of Dan hurt. His insides churned when the man straddled him and came all over his stomach, adding his semen to Stevie's. Something about the intimacy of that act bothered Stevie more than anything had in a while, even Jesse's visit the night before. It felt wrong to come for anyone but Dan, and he hated it.

"Shit, boy, hurry up!" Roy's impatient voice jolted Stevie out of his thoughts. He finished washing himself and dried off with the towel.

Roy picked up the used rags and tossed them in the corner. "Well, reckon that'll have to do."

"Yeah, I'm ready to go out on the fucking town now." Stevie closed his eyes. A yank on his hair made him open them again. Roy's face was inches from his, cold and hard and angrier than Stevie thought he'd ever seen him.

"Now you listen to me, boy, and you listen good." Roy's voice was slow and soft. "You're awful damn close to outlivin' your usefulness. I been gettin' complaints lately. Word'll get around that you ain't worth the money. Don't think you're gettin' out of here alive, if you keep up this shit. The day I stop makin' money on you, that's the day you die. Got it?"

Stevie smiled. "Fuck you, Roy."

Roy bared his tobacco-stained teeth. His free hand shot out and grabbed Stevie around the throat. Stevie lay unresisting. It surprised him a little that the thought of dying comforted him the way it did.

"This is your last chance, boy," Roy said. "You fuck this up, your death wish gonna come true. You think about that."

Roy let go, stood and crossed the room a few strides. He turned back to Stevie as he opened the door. "And if you throw up on another customer, I swear to Jesus I'll cut your balls off."

Roy slammed the door shut behind him. Stevie ignored Roy's threat and laughed quietly to himself at the memory of the night before. The man who'd come in after Jesse had only wanted a blowjob. Normally that would've been an easy one. But the blow to the head had left Stevie feeling horribly sick, and the first latex-flavored thrust down his throat had brought up what little was in his stomach.

The man had not been happy. Stevie had been plenty happy, because his obvious injury had forced Roy to send him to the doctor, whose services Roy used from time to time. It was a mutually beneficial arrangement: stitches, drugs, and HIV testing in exchange for sex and Roy's silence about the doctor's taste for underage boys.

The doctor had said Stevie had a concussion and would have to rest for the remainder of the night if Roy expected him to be able to work later. Roy had cursed and yelled at Stevie for making Jesse hit him, but in the end he hadn't had any choice, and Stevie had spent a night alone for the first time in over a month. He didn't even mind the screaming headache that wouldn't go away because he couldn't keep the pain pills down. Nothing could spoil the luxury of having his time and his body to himself.

When the door opened, rusted hinges protesting, Stevie kept his head turned toward the window. He was vaguely aware of two sets of footsteps entering his room and the door clicking shut again. He closed his eyes and started to withdraw into himself.

"Oh. *Dios mío.*"

Stevie knew that voice. Carlos. His eyes flew open.

Carlos stood just inside the door, eyes fixed on the ceiling, muttering what sounded like curses under his breath in rapid Spanish. Stevie barely registered his presence. Because next to him stood Dan.

Dan, here. In his room. Only Roy had the key to Stevie's room. That could only mean one thing: Dan had paid to get in.

Dan had bought him. Dan had bought him, and he'd brought his straight best friend along to watch.

It was too much. The worst possible humiliation. He still had lots of pills; he could take them all and finally let go. It would be a relief.

Stevie closed his eyes again. Nothing mattered now. Nothing. He lay still and let the coldness inside him well up to numb mind and heart and body.

He didn't react to the shifting of the mattress or the weight next to him. But he couldn't ignore being lifted in Dan's arms, cradled against his body. He opened his eyes and looked up into Dan's face. He was shocked to see the brown eyes filled with anguish.

"Dan?" he whispered. "Why?"

Dan's throat worked. "It was the only way I could get in, Stevie. The cops wouldn't listen, and I couldn't leave you here. Not after I found out." Dan drew a deep, shuddering breath. "I'm so sorry, Stevie. About everything. I'm so damn sorry."

Stevie frowned. This wasn't what he'd expected. He gazed up at Dan with a question he couldn't voice in his eyes. Dan smiled, brushed the dirty, tangled curls away from Stevie's face, and planted a tender kiss on his brow.

"I'm getting you out of here, Stevie," Dan whispered against his hair. "I'm taking you home."

At last, the truth of the situation began to sink in. Dan hadn't bought him at all. Dan had come to rescue him. Again.

Stevie started to tremble. He reached up and wound his arms around Dan's neck, clinging as tight as he could. "Dan. Oh. I thought ... I ... Oh. Oh, God."

Dan held him while a month's worth of savagely suppressed emotion poured out of Stevie in great, ragged sobs. Stevie let it happen, too weak to fight it even if he'd wanted to. He buried his face in Dan's neck and took big, gulping breaths scented with Dan's skin.

Eventually his tears slowed to a trickle, and he lay sniffling in Dan's arms, his head resting on Dan's shoulder. His body felt limp as a rag, and his head screamed with pain, but he felt clean and peaceful for the first time since the day Roy had taken him. Dan had come for him. Dan still loved him. Nothing could compare to that.

"Uh, guys, we should be getting out of here."

Stevie raised his head with a great effort. He'd forgotten all about Carlos.

"Yeah, you're right." Dan lifted Stevie's chin and gently kissed his lips. The heat of that kiss spread like a wave, warming Stevie to his core. The handsome prince bringing the sleeping princess to life with his kiss. The image made Stevie smile. "Stevie, do you have any clothes?"

"No. Roy took 'em all away the first week. So I couldn't leave." Stevie smiled at Dan's stormy expression. "This sure does sound familiar, huh?"

Dan smiled wanly back. "Yeah. Wish it didn't. How bad are you hurt? Can you walk?"

Stevie nodded, carefully because moving his head made him feel queasy. "Pretty sure I can. It's a concussion, is all."

"Shit, Stevie." Dan caressed Stevie's bruised jaw. "Who hit you?"

"Jesse. He bought me last night." Stevie laid his fingers over Dan's lips before he could say a word. "Let it go, Dan. Don't wanna think of him right now."

Dan shook his head. "Okay. But I won't forget. He's going to jail right along with that son of a bitch Roy, if I've got anything to say about it." Dan set Stevie gently back on the bed and stood up.

"We've got about forty minutes before the hour's up," Carlos said. He was rummaging through the tiny closet with its built-in shelves. "Shit. Not a damn thing in here but junk." He turned to look at Stevie. "We can't take you out naked, Stevie."

Dan shrugged out of his jacket. "Here, put this on." He helped Stevie into the jacket. The sleeves hung a good six inches past Stevie's hands, and the leather was soft and warm and smelled like Dan. Stevie clutched it around him.

"Whoa, hang on." Carlos stood on tiptoe, reached to the back of the top shelf, and pulled out a lump of paint-splattered denim. He shook it out, sending a cloud of dust into the air. "Somebody's old work jeans. Look like they've been here forever, but it's better than nothing."

"Carlos, you're amazing," Dan said. "Hand those over."

Carlos tossed the jeans to Dan. Dan caught them and knelt at Stevie's feet. He tugged the worn, dirty garment up Stevie's legs. Stevie clung to Dan's arm and stood on shaky legs to pull the pants the rest of the way up. He wound an arm around Dan's waist and leaned against him. The jeans stayed on, though they clung precariously to his hipbones and dragged the floor under his feet.

"All right, guess we're ready as we can get," Dan said. "Stevie?"

Stevie nodded against Dan's chest. "Yeah, I'm ready. Let's hurry, huh? Don't feel so good."

Carlos cracked the door open and peered out. "Coast is clear, for now. Come on."

They eased into the hall and toward the front stairs, Stevie clinging to Dan for balance. His head throbbed, and dizziness made his steps falter. It seemed to take forever to reach the stairs. Carlos went down far enough to check the downstairs hall, then beckoned them to follow.

"Just where the fuck you think you're goin'?"

Roy's voice stopped them just short of the front door. Stevie dug his fingers into Dan's waist and held on while Dan turned them to face Roy.

"We're leaving," Dan said. "I'm taking him out of here."

Roy laughed as he walked toward them. "The hell you say. That boy ain't goin' no place 'cept back upstairs."

Stevie glanced toward the front room. It was empty except for one scrawny boy and the elderly man whose lap he was straddling. Neither even looked up. Stevie held himself as straight as he could and looked Roy in the eye.

"I'm going home, Roy," he said.

"Home? You ain't got a home, boy." Roy gave Stevie a disdainful look, then glared up at Dan. "Now you just let go of that kid and get the fuck out of here. Don't know what you want with him anyhow; little shit ain't even worth what you paid."

Dan's jaw clenched. He gently pried Stevie's fingers loose and took a step toward Roy. Stevie put out a hand to steady himself, and Carlos took it. They glanced at each other. Stevie saw his own concern mirrored in Carlos's eyes. Dan could easily kill Roy with his bare hands. Unless Roy was armed. Stevie didn't much like the possibilities there.

"Mister," Dan growled, stalking toward Roy, "you haven't got a fucking clue what Stevie's worth to me. He doesn't work for you anymore. And he does have a home, and that home's with me. I'm taking him back now, and you're not stopping me."

Roy grinned. He opened his mouth, probably to call for his enforcers. Dan was on him before he could make a sound, wrapping both big hands around Roy's neck. Roy's eyes bulged, fingers scrabbling at Dan's hands as Dan lifted him nearly off his feet. Stevie could barely hear Dan when he spoke, but the cold fury in Dan's voice send a chill through him.

"You shut the fuck up," Dan hissed. "I oughta kill you right now. God knows I want to. We're leaving now. And if you ever lay one filthy finger on Stevie again, you're dead. Remember that."

Dan slammed Roy's head against the wall and let him drop, gasping, to the floor.

"Hey, what's going on?" The boy from the front room stood in the doorway, pale blue eyes wide in his white face. He glanced from Roy to Dan in confusion, then stepped hesitantly toward Dan.

"I wouldn't, *chico*," Carlos said. The boy paled at the look on Dan's face. He gulped and backed up again.

Stevie's stomach churned. The room whirled around him, and his vision blurred. He managed to gasp, "Dan, 'm gonna be sick," before falling to his knees and throwing up.

After a few seconds, the heaving stopped, and the fierce pain in his skull eased a little. Dan knelt beside him, stroking his hair, his face, his back. It felt good.

"Hey, Stevie," Carlos said. "You gave Roy a little something to remember you by."

Stevie looked and started laughing. He'd managed to throw up all over Roy's legs, where the bastard lay slumped against the wall. He leaned closer. "Hey, Roy, I didn't puke on the customers this time, you piece of shit."

It said a lot about how dazed Roy was that he didn't even manage his usual glare. Stevie was almost disappointed.

Before Dan stood up, he reached into Roy's shirt pocket and pulled out the money he'd given him for Sunshine. As he rose, he held a hand down to Stevie. "I wasn't happy with the service here, Roy, so I'm getting my money back. Come on, Stevie, let's get out of here."

"Hell, yeah."

Stevie let Dan help him to his feet. The world went dark for a second. When he surfaced again, Stevie found himself being carried out the door. The night air was icy and sharp and winter clean. Stevie smiled against Dan's chest and let himself drift away.

CHAPTER SEVENTEEN

Carlos took Dan's keys and drove straight to the hospital. Dan bundled Stevie into the back seat and climbed in beside him, laying Stevie's head on his thigh. About halfway there, Stevie woke up long enough to climb into Dan's lap and curl up against him before falling asleep again. Dan held him, kissing his hair and caressing his bare skin under the jacket. He traced Stevie's protruding ribs with his fingers and wished he'd killed Roy when he had the chance.

The emergency room triage nurse took one look at Stevie, bruised and half-conscious in Dan's arms, and led them straight back to an examination room. Dan laid Stevie gently on the table.

Stevie's eyes fluttered open. "Dan, don't leave me." He clutched at Dan's hand.

"I won't." Dan took Stevie's hand, kissed his fingers. "I love you."

Stevie smiled. "Love you, too. Missed you so much, Dan."

Dan sat in the chair beside the stretcher and leaned his forehead against Stevie's. Seconds later, a nurse came in and spent a brisk few minutes checking vital signs, asking Stevie questions, and making him follow her finger with his eyes.

"The doctor'll be here in a minute," she said. "After she's had a look at you, Stevie, I can bring you something for your head."

"Oh, yeah, that'd be good," Stevie said. He rolled onto his side and went back to sleep.

"I should go call Shawna," Carlos said as the nurse left the room.

"Yeah, she's probably worried. Would you see if she'd call Melina for me?"

"Sure thing." Carlos squeezed Dan's shoulder. "Should I call the cops, too?"

Dan considered. "I don't know. I don't want to make Stevie have to talk to them until he's ready." He ran a finger down Stevie's cheek. "Stevie? Wake up a minute, baby."

"Hm?" Stevie mumbled without opening his eyes.

"We need to call the cops, Stevie. You feel like talking to them tonight or you want to wait?"

Stevie wrinkled his nose. "Let's get it over with. Roy'll have the whole place cleaned out if I wait."

"All right." Dan leaned down and kissed Stevie's cheek, then turned back to Carlos. "Yeah, go on and call them. I sure as hell hope they listen this time."

Carlos smiled grimly. "They'll have to. They can't blow off all three of us."

Carlos headed to the waiting room to make the calls. Dan sat and held Stevie's hand while they waited for the doctor. He hoped Carlos was right.

* * * * *

The police showed up about an hour later. Stevie related his story in a calm, neutral voice, then Dan and Carlos reported their own experiences. Dan kept his face carefully blank as Stevie talked, but it killed something inside him to hear how Stevie had been treated. His heart nearly stopped when Stevie said that Roy had threatened to kill him. He pressed Stevie's hand to his cheek and thanked whatever powers existed that he'd gotten him out in time.

"Okay, I think we have enough to make an arrest." The detective snapped his small notebook shut and gave Stevie a sharp look. "Make sure you don't leave town; we may need to get in touch with you. Mr. Corazon, Mr. Hernandez, that goes for you, too."

"No problem," Carlos said.

Dan glanced at Stevie; he looked exhausted, his eyes already drifting closed again. "We won't leave town. But I can take him home once the doc releases him, right?"

"Yes, that's fine. Here's my card. Call if you think of anything else we need to know, okay?"

"Okay. Thanks, Detective." Dan took the business card the man held out. "What about Jesse? Can you arrest him, too?"

The detective nodded. "Yes, absolutely. If you want to press charges, that is, Mr. Sanger."

Stevie opened his eyes and looked up at the detective. "Yeah, I do."

"Okay, we'll haul him in, too."

Dan and Carlos shook hands with the detective before he left. Stevie was already asleep again.

* * * * *

They ended up spending nearly six hours in the emergency room. After blood work and a brain scan, the doctor confirmed that Stevie had a concussion, adding that he was dehydrated and malnourished. So Stevie lay on the narrow ER stretcher and slept on and off while the nurses gave him vitamin-infused fluids through an IV tube. They wanted him to eat, but he refused, saying he still felt sick. The medication they gave him for the headache and nausea made him feel better, but it left him so groggy he could barely keep his eyes open, let alone manage to eat anything. Eventually the nurse left Dan with a can of soda and some crackers, and instructions to give Stevie some of it any time he was awake enough.

Dawn was breaking when they finally left. Dan pocketed the prescriptions, a doctor's appointment card, and the list of instructions, and helped Stevie back into his jacket while Carlos went to get the Jeep. Stevie already looked better, even though he kept falling asleep whenever no one was speaking directly to him. That worried Dan a little, but the doctor and nurses assured him it was not unusual, and told him not to worry unless Stevie became confused or wouldn't wake up.

The ride back home was much like the ride to the hospital: Carlos driving, Dan in the back seat with Stevie huddled in the curve of his arm. When they arrived home, Stevie flatly refused to let Dan carry him up the stairs to the apartment, insisting he felt strong enough to walk up himself.

This turned out to be half true. He did walk up, with Dan on one side and Carlos on the other, supporting him. By the time they reached the third floor, Stevie's face was set in lines of pain. His heart pounded so hard Dan could feel it against his arm. For the first time since he'd lived there, Dan wished the building had an elevator. He breathed a sigh of relief when they finally reached his apartment. They deposited Stevie on the sofa, where he curled up without a word. Carlos tossed Dan's keys on the counter.

Dan turned to Carlos. "Thanks, Carlos. For everything."

Carlos hugged him hard. "You'd do the same, Danny. Love you, *hermano*."

"Love you, too, man."

Stevie pushed himself to a sitting position and held his arms up. "C'mere, Carlos."

Carlos laughed, bent, and hugged Stevie. "Glad you're okay, bro."

Stevie gazed up at him, his expression serious. "Roy really was gonna kill me, you know. You and Dan saved my life. Thanks for doing that."

"Hey, you and Danny are family. Families take care of each other." Carlos gently ruffled Stevie's curls. "I better go. Don't be surprised if Shawna stops by later. She's dying to fuss over you, Stevie."

Stevie laughed, then groaned in obvious pain, holding his head in both hands. "Aw, damn. Everything fucking hurts. She can come over, sure, I wanna see her, too. I missed her."

"I'll tell her to wait awhile, so you can get some sleep." Carlos headed for the door. "'Bye, guys. Later."

Dan and Stevie both called good-bye and thank you to Carlos as he left. Dan moved to the door and turned the deadbolt. He went back to Stevie and sat down beside him. Stevie promptly snuggled against him. Dan thought he could be happy just living this moment forever, with Stevie warm and real and safe in his arms.

"You must be worn out," Dan said after several long minutes. "Why don't we go on to bed, huh?"

Stevie nodded. "Yeah, I feel like I could sleep for a year." He raised his head from Dan's shoulder and pulled back enough to look him in the eye. "But, can I take a bath first? I feel dirty."

"Sure you can, if that's what you want. I'll help you." Dan lifted Stevie's chin and kissed him.

The kiss was long and slow and so, so gentle. The feel of Stevie's fingers in his hair made Dan's skin tingle. He reluctantly broke the kiss after a few minutes, before his body started wanting things it couldn't have just yet.

"Come on, baby," Dan said. "Let's get you washed up, then you can sleep as long as you want."

Stevie smiled, tracing Dan's jaw with his fingers. "Sounds great. I love you, Dan."

"I love you, too." Dan kissed Stevie's nose. "C'mon."

In the bathroom, Dan flipped the heater on and started the water running while he helped Stevie undress. When the water was high enough, he helped Stevie step into the tub, stripped his own shirt off, and started washing him. He lathered Stevie's hair, working his fingers gently through the tangles, then rinsed it with clean water from the tap. The way the golden strands straightened and curled in the flowing water fascinated him.

Dan soaped and rinsed Stevie's body, using his palm instead of the washcloth on the raw skin of his thighs and buttocks. Stevie grimaced in obvious pain, but didn't say anything. Afterward, Dan helped him out of the tub and patted him dry with the softest towel he could find.

"There," Dan said, drying Stevie's hair as best he could with the towel. "All clean. You think you can stand up long enough for me to put some antibiotic ointment on those cuts?"

"I think so." Stevie wound his arms around Dan's waist and pressed against him. "Thank you, Dan."

"For what?" Dan kissed Stevie's damp hair.

"For taking care of me like this."

"Oh, baby, don't thank me." Dan lifted Stevie's face and stared down into those blue eyes. "I will gladly spend the rest of my life making up for what I did to you."

Tears welled in Stevie's eyes. "We both made mistakes, Dan. You don't owe me anything. Let's start over, huh? Clean slate."

Dan smiled. "I'd like that."

* * * * *

It took a few minutes for Dan to coat all of Stevie's cuts with ointment. Stevie's legs were shaking by the time he finished. Dan held Stevie up while he brushed his teeth, then they made their way to the bedroom. Dan dressed Stevie in soft cotton pajamas and tucked him under the covers. He fetched a glass of water and gave Stevie one of each of the pills the hospital had given him for pain and nausea, making a mental note to go to the drug store and get the prescriptions filled the next day. The hospital had only given him enough to last twenty-four hours.

Dan kissed Stevie's cheek before going back to the bathroom to brush his own teeth, and by the time he got back, Stevie was sound asleep, curled up in a ball. He looked like a little boy in Dan's oversized pajamas. Dan smiled, stripped off his jeans, and crawled under the covers wearing just his boxers. He pulled Stevie close. Stevie cuddled against him without waking up, curling his body around Dan's. He fit perfectly in Dan's arms. Dan drifted into his first peaceful sleep in weeks, washed in the scent of Stevie's skin.

CHAPTER EIGHTEEN

In Stevie's dream, he and Dan made love in the tall yellow grass of their own secret meadow. The sun's heat pressed like a weight under a deep-cerulean sky. Stevie's happiness flowed from him in rivers of light, illuminating Dan's face as they loved each other.

When consciousness started tugging at him, he fought it just as he always did. Dan's loving smile blurred behind a veil of tears, the light of Stevie's joy fading into despair. The meadow went gray, he was ripped from Dan's arms, and he screamed ...

... and the dream shattered around him. He sat bolt upright in bed, shaking all over. The air rang with the echo of his cry. He reached out, swallowing panic. And Dan was there, Dan's arms were around him, warm and solid and very real. Dan pulled him close, rubbing his back in soothing circles.

"Stevie, it's okay, baby," Dan whispered against his hair. "It's okay. Just a bad dream, is all."

Stevie rested his head in the curve of Dan's neck, letting Dan's nearness comfort him. "The dream was beautiful. We were back in the meadow, making love in the grass. I was so happy."

"What scared you, then?" Dan lay back down, taking Stevie with him. Stevie snuggled against Dan's chest.

"When Roy had me, I dreamed of you every time I went to sleep. And I knew I was dreaming, and I hated waking up, because I'd have to leave you. I fought it so hard, but I never could stay asleep. I always woke up, and I was in that awful place." Stevie raised his head enough to look into Dan's eyes. "In my dream this time, I thought I'd wake up and still be at Roy's place. I didn't remember. And I thought I'd never see you again."

Dan's eyes gazed sorrowfully back at him. "Oh, baby. I'm so sorry."

Stevie smiled. "You're real this time, Dan. You're really here."

"That's right. You won't ever have to wake up alone and scared again." Dan laid a hand on Stevie's cheek and kissed him. "Love you so much."

"Love you, Dan." Stevie slipped a hand under Dan's head, leaned down, and returned the kiss.

One gentle kiss led to another, and another, and another, each a little deeper than the one before, a little more heated. Desire rose between them, building at an unhurried pace into a quietly simmering need. They pulled back at the same time and stared into each other's eyes.

"Touch me," Stevie whispered.

Dan ran a thumb over Stevie's lips. "You sure?"

"Yes. I need you to, Dan." Stevie took Dan's hand and laid it over his erection. He could feel the heat of Dan's palm through the thin pajama bottoms. "Please."

Dan groaned. "Yeah. God, I missed touching you."

They undressed each other, taking time for kisses and caresses as they went. Naked, they wound their bodies together, hands mapping each other, learning each other all over again, mouths locked in a deep kiss. Stevie shuddered as Dan's cock pressed against his, making him burn all over. He moaned into Dan's mouth.

Dan wrapped one big hand around both their cocks. Stevie twined his fingers with Dan's, and together they stroked the two shafts. Dan's cock was a sweet, silken friction against Stevie's, sending deep pulses of pleasure through his bones. He rolled his hips, pushing into their joined hands.

Stevie wanted to lose himself forever in the feel of Dan's fingers, his cock, his burning kiss. Dan broke the kiss just as Stevie felt the pressure inside him approach the point of no return.

"Come for me, Stevie," Dan gasped. "Wanna see."

Stevie did, eyes locked with Dan's as a fierce, toe-curling orgasm tore through him. Dan came seconds after Stevie, his body shaking in Stevie's arms.

Stevie's eyes burned. He buried his face in Dan's neck, stifling a sob.

Dan's fingers raked through Stevie's hair. "Stevie, you okay?"

Stevie raised his head, blinking back the tears that didn't want to stop. Dan wiped them away. "Stevie? What's wrong?"

Stevie shook his head. He could feel his old, automatic smile slipping into place. "It's nothing. I'm just tired, is all. I'm fine."

Dan cupped Stevie's face in his hands. "Don't hide from me, baby," he whispered. "It's okay to cry. You've sure as hell got a right to, after all you've been through."

Stevie stared into Dan's eyes, and something inside him shifted. Dan accepted all of him, loved him completely, in spite of the ugly truths of his past. He didn't have to hide what he felt from Dan. He'd never had to. He laid his cheek against Dan's chest and cried, for all the pain he'd left behind and all the happiness to come. When the tears dried and he drifted to sleep again, safe in Dan's arms, he didn't dream.

* * * * *

Stevie slept through most of Sunday. He woke gradually in the late afternoon, to the soft murmur of voices in the next room. He smiled when he recognized Shawna's laugh.

He sat up, stretched, and climbed carefully out of bed. He stood there for a moment, assessing how he felt. The monstrous pain in his skull had faded to a dull ache, and the dizziness was gone altogether. He was surprised to find that not only did he not feel like throwing up anymore, he was actually hungry. He put on Dan's pajama bottoms, pulling the drawstring snug so they wouldn't fall off, and wandered out into the living room.

Dan saw him first, followed almost immediately by Carlos and Shawna when Dan's huge smile alerted them. Dan jumped up, put an arm around Stevie's shoulders, and led him to a chair at the table in the kitchen.

"Hey, sleeping beauty," Shawna said, grinning. She jumped up and hugged him. "Damn, it's good to see you."

"You too, gorgeous." Stevie returned her hug. "I missed you."

"How you feeling?" Dan asked, brushing the hair from Stevie's eyes. "Better?"

"Lots," Stevie said. He lifted his face to Dan's. Dan kissed him, then sat down beside him, lacing their fingers together.

"You sure look better," Carlos said.

"I'd about have to, huh?" Stevie leaned his head on Dan's shoulder. "I'm hungry, Dan, what've we got to eat?"

Shawna piped up before Dan could do more than draw breath. "I made muffins, if you feel up to it. Apple cinnamon."

Just the thought made Stevie's mouth water. "Oh, man. That sounds perfect."

"Hang on, I'll get them for you." Shawna jumped up and hurried into the kitchen.

"What'd I say, bro?" Carlos chuckled. "Fussing like a mother hen."

Stevie laughed. "Hey, I'll let her pamper me 'til she gets sick of it, no problem."

"I called John and Evan this morning," Dan said. "John about jumped through the phone when I told him you were home. They want to know when they can come see you."

Stevie took a muffin from the plate Shawna brought to the table at that moment and gave Dan a wide-eyed look as he peeled the paper off. "You mean they're not mad at me? For leaving them in the lurch like I did?"

"Nope." Dan helped himself to a muffin while Shawna set a glass of orange juice down in front of Stevie. "They don't know the whole story, but they know something happened between us before you left, and they're not mad. They want you to come back to work soon as you feel up to it."

"Oh, wow." Stevie talked through a mouthful of muffin. "Oh, man, I can't even tell you how glad I am to hear that."

"And," Dan continued, "Roy's in jail. That detective called earlier to let us know. He thinks they may be able to get the judge to deny bail, too, so with any luck we won't have to worry about him at all until his trial. And with all the evidence they say they've got, it looks like he might not see the light of day for a long time."

"Oh, my God." Stevie popped the rest of the muffin into his mouth, chewed and swallowed, then scooted onto Dan's lap, snagging a second muffin as he went. "You know what? I think everything's gonna be all right now."

"I think you're right." Dan wrapped his arms around Stevie, holding him securely against his chest. "Welcome home, babe."

Stevie leaned back and met Dan's lips with his. The kiss was alive with promise. Stevie smiled as they pulled apart.

"Dan," he said. "It's good to be home."

Dan sat behind the wheel of his Jeep, squirming with impatience. Friday afternoon traffic was always heavy, but early June seemed to be a particularly busy time, almost as bad as leaf season. He resisted the urge to honk his horn at the white-haired woman peering through the steering wheel of the Cadillac in front of him. He made it through the light just before it turned red, and let out the breath he'd been holding.

He turned into the Rainbow Books parking lot and parked in the only available space, near the back under a huge old willow. He jumped out and practically ran across the parking lot. His heart pounded with more than the usual excitement of seeing Stevie again after a long day at work. The news he was dying to tell had him grinning from ear to ear as he pushed open the door and hurried in.

"Hi, Dan!" John called from the register. He handed a bag full of books to a young woman with three small children in tow, patted her arm, and smiled at Dan as he sauntered over. "You look like the cat that got the canary, sweetie, what's up?"

"Got some news. Where're Stevie and Evan? I want to tell everybody at once."

"Stevie's back at the coffee shop. Evan's in the back office, as usual. What ..." John's eyes went wide. "Oh, my lord. Is it what I think? Please tell me it is."

Dan nodded. "Sure is. He got ..."

"Don't tell me!" John interrupted. He hurried around the counter, grabbed Dan's hand, and tugged him toward the coffee shop. "Come on, we'll find our men, and you can break the news all at once."

Dan laughed. "Okay."

"Megan!" John called to the pretty brunette busy wiping down tables. "Could you work the register for me for a few minutes, hon?"

"Sure, John." She tossed the paper towel she was using in the trash and headed toward the front. "Hey, Dan."

"Hey, Megan," Dan said. He smiled at her back as she walked off. "Sweet girl."

"Oh, honey, she's been a lifesaver," John laughed. "Stevie! Come out, come out, wherever you are, sugar! Dan's here!"

A few of the people waiting in line for coffee and desserts smiled indulgently at John. Others ignored him completely. Dan laughed.

"Dan!" Stevie appeared from the small kitchen in back of the counter. He wiped his hands on his purple apron and smiled as he came around front. "Hey, baby."

Dan opened his arms and swept Stevie into a hug, lifting him right off his feet. He gave Stevie a light kiss as he put him down again.

"Hey," Dan said. "How're things here? Looks like business is good."

"Oh, man, it's insane." Stevie laughed. "I love it."

"Best thing we ever did, opening this coffee shop," John added. "It's been open, what, a week now, and we're already getting a lot more business because of it. It's Stevie's cookies and pies and stuff. They're to die for."

"You got that right." Dan grinned down at Stevie. "Can you get away for a few minutes, babe? I got some news."

Stevie's face went dead white. "Oh, shit. Um. Okay, yeah."

Stevie turned around, keeping a death grip on Dan's hand. "Hey, Sarah," he called to the young woman taking orders at the counter, "I'm going to talk to Dan for a few minutes, okay? Be back in a little bit."

Sarah nodded and waved. Dan wrapped an arm around Stevie's shoulders as they headed toward Evan's office. He could feel Stevie trembling.

"Don't worry," Dan whispered. "It's good."

Stevie gave him a grateful smile.

Evan was frowning at a spreadsheet when John swept into the office, followed by Dan and Stevie. He looked up, eyebrows raised. "Yes?"

"Dan has some news, and he wanted to tell all of us together," John announced. He gave Dan a little push forward. "Go ahead, sweetie."

Dan pulled Stevie closer and kissed the top of his head. "Got a call just a little while ago from the DA's office. They sentenced Roy today."

The little room went perfectly still. Stevie had sat down with John and Evan as soon as he went back to work and told them the whole story: his history as a prostitute, how Dan had found him, his kidnapping and rescue. Both men were nearly as anxious as Dan and Stevie to see Roy sent to prison. The guilty verdict on a host of charges had been cause enough for celebration, but they'd all been waiting anxiously for the sentencing.

Stevie stared up at Dan, blue eyes huge. "What'd he get?"

Dan smiled. "Life without parole."

A heartbeat of silence. Then Stevie let out a wild whoop and leapt into Dan's arms, wrapping arms and legs around him. Dan swung him around, laughing.

"Oh, man, that's great!" Stevie gave Dan an enthusiastic kiss.

"It was the murder that put him over the top, I think." Dan set Stevie on his feet again. They kept their arms around each other. "I mean all the other stuff was bad enough, but I'm thinking the murder did the bastard in."

Two of Roy's boys had testified to helping him kill the man who had bought Stevie the night before Dan found him. Roy had tried to beat the man into confessing that he'd killed Stevie. When the man kept insisting he hadn't, Roy had lost patience and shot him in the head. The police had found his body right where the boys had said it would be.

"Yes, that would do it," Evan mused. "So what all charges did he end up with?"

"First-degree murder, kidnapping, arson, and several counts of aggravated assault, plus all the charges from his prostitution business."

"God, I feel a thousand pounds lighter. No more Roy! All that shit's totally behind me now." Stevie laughed, bouncing in place with excitement. "Party at our place tonight! Yeah!"

Dan laughed with him, tilted his chin up, and gave him a quick kiss. "I'll call Melina and Aaron. Carlos already knows, he was there with me when I got the call. He's probably already talked to Shawna."

"We'll bring the booze," John offered. He squeezed Stevie's hand as they all headed out of the office. "I'm so happy for you, honey. You go on home with Dan, we'll see you tonight."

"Okay, thanks."

Stevie gave John and Evan each a fierce hug, then bounded over the coffee shop to tell Sarah he was leaving. He ran into the back and came out minus the flour-strewn apron. Dan smiled at him as they left the bookstore arm in arm.

"I'm glad it's all over with now," Dan said. "It's been a tough few months, huh?"

Stevie nodded. Dan could see the stress of Roy's trial in his eyes. Testifying against Roy had been emotional torture for Stevie. Roy's lawyer had used every weapon at her disposal, including all the sordid details of Stevie's past. Dan had wanted to strangle her when she told the entire courtroom that Stevie had been kicked out of college and disowned by his wealthy family and why. Stevie had endured it all with a calmness and grace that made Dan ache with pride. No one but Dan knew how many nights Stevie had cried himself to sleep.

"The trial's been hell," Stevie agreed. "But it was worth it." He stopped just outside the door of the shop, wound his arms around Dan's waist, and gazed up into his eyes. "And I've had you to help me through it. I couldn't have made it without you, Dan."

"I hate you've had to go through all this, baby." Dan cupped Stevie's face in his hands, letting his fingers trace the silky skin.

Stevie rubbed his cheek against Dan's palm. "It wasn't easy. But nothing worthwhile ever is."

Snapshots of the past eleven months flitted through Dan's mind. Not quite a year, but in that short time he'd become a different person. Shedding his old self had been both the hardest and the best thing he'd ever done. And the reward for all that hard work was smiling in his arms, blue eyes bright with hope.

He raised Stevie's face and gave him a long, deep, lingering kiss. "Don't I know it."

ABOUT THE AUTHOR

Ally is a married mother of two, living in the mountains of North Carolina in the U.S.A. She is a registered nurse by trade and a writer of man-love by inclination. Her husband is a freelance artist, and their children have apparently inherited his artistic tendencies. Thankfully, they have also inherited his singing voice instead of Ally's, which her family will confirm can peel the paint off the walls.

Ally wrote her first story — a slash fanfic — in the fall of 2003. She has since branched out into original character gay romance. Her short stories have been published in the e-zines Forbidden Fruit and Ruthie's Club, and her novels are available from Loose Id and Samhain Publishing.

In addition to writing, Ally enjoys traveling, collecting dragons, and trying to scare herself. Her favorite authors include Stephen King, Clive Barker, and Laurell K. Hamilton, and she is a rabid fan of horror movies.

Ally adores music, particularly Radiohead and Patrick Wolf. She plans to have her iPod surgically implanted as soon as someone invents a way to do that. Hopefully this will mean the end of playing CDs and her children can finally stop telling her to turn the volume down.

Visit Ally on the Web at http://www.allyblue.com.

Stimulate yourself.
READ.
www.manloveromance.com
THE HOTTEST M/M EROTIC AUTHORS & WEBSITES ON THE NET

Printed in the United States
144507LV00001B/8/P

9 781934 531624